The Story of China's Persecuted Church, Vol.2

EXILES
OF HOPE

The Story of China's Persecuted Church, Vol.2

EXILES OF HOPE

ANTHONY G. BOLLBACK

Pleasant Word
A Division of WINEPRESS PUBLISHING

© 2005 by Anthony G. Bollback. All rights reserved

Pleasant Word (a division of WinePress Publishing, PO Box 428, Enumclaw, WA 98022) functions only as book publisher. As such, the ultimate design, content, editorial accuracy, and views expressed or implied in this work are those of the author.

No part of this publication may be reproduced, stored in a retrieval system or transmitted in any way by any means—electronic, mechanical, photocopy, recording or otherwise—without the prior permission of the copyright holder, except as provided by USA copyright law.

Unless otherwise noted, all Scriptures are taken from the Holy Bible, New International Version, Copyright © 1973, 1978, 1984 by the International Bible Society. Used by permission of Zondervan Publishing House. The "NIV" and "New International Version" trademarks are registered in the United States Patent and Trademark Office by International Bible Society.

Scripture references marked KJV are taken from the King James Version of the Bible.

Scripture references marked NASB are taken from the New American Standard Bible, © 1960, 1963, 1968, 1971, 1972, 1973, 1975, 1977 by The Lockman Foundation. Used by permission.

ISBN 1-4141-0384-0
Library of Congress Catalog Card Number: 2005900561

DEDICATION

In loving memory of Joshua, the pastor of the Wuchang Church,
characterized in this book as "Pastor Yang,"
whose real name is withheld here to protect his family.

He was my dear friend—
a faithful and committed servant of God
who spent twenty years of his life working as a prisoner in a
stone quarry
because of his faith in Jesus Christ.
He turned those long years of internment
into victory through Jesus Christ
and lived to see the fulfillment of the vision God had given him
of a thriving Bible Seminary in Wuchang.

I waited patiently for the LORD;
And He inclined to me,
And heard my cry.
He also brought me up out of a horrible pit,
Out of the miry clay;
And set my feet upon a rock,
And established my steps.
He has put a new song in my mouth—
Praise to our God;
Many will see it and fear,
And will trust in the LORD."
(Psalm 40:1-3)

TABLE OF CONTENTS

INTRODUCTION

No place on earth resembles the Book of Acts more closely than the church in China today. It has mushroomed from fewer than two million believers in 1949 to more than eighty million. And this dynamic growth has happened during years when churches were closed, when Bibles were banned and burned, when thousands of believers were imprisoned and killed, and when no missionaries remained in the country. Without question God has been at work in China in the most amazing demonstration of the power of the Holy Spirit taking place in any country of the world today.

At the time when *Red Runs the River: The Story of China's Persecuted Church, Volume One*, was released in March, 2004, it was difficult for me to anticipate the response. I was excited to receive accounts of people coming to Christ, making new commitments for service, and renewing their passion for prayer. As a result of many letters, I soon realized that this book was perhaps the culmination of my life's work among the Chinese people.

Letter-writers urged me to complete *Volume Two* as soon as possible, not merely so that readers could learn the outcome of the years of separation of Meiling and Anching, the first book's two main characters, but because people were touched by its message.

Encouraged by the response, I began *Volume Two: Exiles of Hope*, with the prayer that God would continue to use this story to stir the Western Church to repentance and action.

Since August of 2004 those of us who live in Florida have been pounded by four hurricanes (all within a period of six weeks.) During two long periods of mandatory evacuations because of the hurricanes, I had some uninterrupted time to complete the writing of this book. What struck me most vividly was that these storms caused us personal loss of property and great inconvenience, but in comparison to my Chinese brothers and sisters, who at times have lost everything for their faith, we've suffered so little. They suffered the loss of all things for Christ, and they did it without complaint. My earnest prayer is simply that God will use this second volume to continue to inspire people to follow the example of the church in China and to love Jesus supremely. Only then will the church awaken from its lethargy.

Like *Volume One* of this story, *Exiles of Hope* relies on authentic and verifiable accounts of believers who lived through the horrendous period of persecution from 1949 to 1985, when the Communists ruthlessly subjugated the populace with harsh and cruel treatment. They discovered, however, that Christians were people of hope, and because of Jesus, they found victory over every obstacle.

Exiles of Hope graphically reveals the importance of Scripture in the life of these believers and how much they were willing to sacrifice in order to have access to even a small portion of the Bible. Although denied their freedom and tortured unmercifully, these Christians continued to place their hope in God.

Let me include one cultural note as our story begins. Typically the Western Church is unaccustomed to the way God reveals Himself to seeking people in Asia and the Muslim world today. In those regions there are a multitude of verifiable incidents of God revealing Himself to people in dreams and visions. Some may question these experiences, but it must be remembered that unlike the West many of those in the East have no Bible or only small portions of Scripture. In both volumes of this story, and particularly in Volume Two, there are several instances where God revealed an urgent message to believers, especially in times of danger.

As believers obeyed the leading of the Lord, some very unusual things happened, and under most difficult circumstances. These incidents are not the figment of my imagination; they are things that actually happened as believers trusted in the Lord completely. In no instance are the dreams associated with revelations of new truth, for God has fully revealed Himself in Scripture and nothing else can be added; rather, they are instances where God gave guidance to His trusting and obedient followers. The most important lesson for all, however, whether living in the East or the West, is that God expects His people to obey Him when He reveals Himself.

I am deeply grateful to my wife, Evelyn, for her prayers, encouragement, suggestions, and willingness to allow me uninterrupted time to complete the writing of this book. My daughter, Joy Peters, once again has been my editor and advisor. What a blessing she has been as she has used her gifts to serve God and to make this book one that would speak to the hearts of young and old alike. To my dear friends, Bob and Millie Wyllie, I say "thank you" for your advice and encouragement to me during the writing of this book.

May *Exiles of Hope* enable you to live victoriously despite your trials and sufferings and teach you to lean your full weight on Jesus Christ. May it open new vistas of service and fruitful living as you fully commit yourself even more fully to God!

Anthony G. Bollback
Kissimmee, Florida,
January 2005

WHAT OTHERS ARE SAYING

Recently I saw a banner across the front of a church in Asia, announcing a new program: "Acts 29." It could very well have been referring to Exiles of Hope. Truly the Acts of the Holy Spirit continue as Jesus builds His Church in China. Anthony Bollback has captured that in this moving sequel to *Red Runs the River*, which will result in greater praise to God, prayers for Chinese believers, and inspiration for the reader.

Dr. David E. Schroeder
President
Nyack College / Alliance Theology Seminary

Exiles of Hope expresses the bold and resolved witness of China's house-church Christians. The characters in this story challenge the reader to exchange temporal, earthly comforts for eternal, heavenly glory as they risk imprisonment and torture to tell others about the greatest story ever told—the death and resurrection of Jesus Christ,

Dr. Tom White
Director of The Voice of the Martyrs–U.S.A.

Exiles of Hope is fascinating! This true-to-life historical novel will encourage those who faithfully prayed for the church in China when little or no news filtered through the "bamboo curtain." I wholeheartedly recommend it to every Christian.

Dr. Charles W. Shepson,
Founder of Fairhaven Ministries,
Roan Mountain, TN

Introduction

Here is an incredibly amazing story of real people who suffered beyond measure for the Lord. Their hope was in the Lord and His Word, and they refused to bend their knee to the evil forces of Communism. It is told in such a wonderful way by my brother who lived there and knew these people. Honestly, it is a humbling experience to read this book and then look at our commitment to the Lord.

Dr. Harry Bollback
Senior Director, Word of Life International,
Schroon Lake, NY

With enormous spiritual and practical application, Anthony Bollback, once again captures the essence of the fears and joys of serving God in another cultural setting with one overarching theme that all things work together for good to those who love Him. In practical and miraculous ways, the reader senses that God is always behind the scenes—guiding, protecting, providing, and blessing His children. Exiles of Hope encourages and empowers every Christian on his or her journey with God. It is compelling, action packed, and heart pounding in human drama … a must read if you want to regain the wonder of your walk with God.

Dr. Mark T. O'Farrell
District Superintendent, Southeastern District
The Christian and Missionary Alliance

Exiles of Hope is a most welcome addition to the first volume of *The Story of China's Persecuted Church.* The expansion of the Chinese church in the second half of the twentieth century is one of the great events of Christian history. Persecution, suffering and martyrdom has not stunted the Church, but has been the occasion for the miraculous response of the Chinese people to the message of Christ's love. Using fiction as a vehicle and out of his rich background experience as missionary, pastor and church administrator, Anthony Bollback vividly and sensitively captures the reality of this phenomenal movement of the Holy Spirit without compromising the safety of those portrayed in the story.

Dr. Rexford A. Boda
Past President of Canadian Bible College/Canadian Theological Seminary, and Nyack College/Alliance Theological Seminary

"Meiling screamed as the searing pain of an electric prod was suddenly thrust against her body.... She was pushed forward to a cell and violently shoved to the floor as the door clanged shut.... Roused by a guard, she was taken, her hair disheveled and face bloodied, to an interrogation room. 'How many times must you be warned to cease your Christian activities?'... Meiling stood quietly, not uttering a word. Grabbing the electric prod, the guard forced her to her knees, sending a surge through her mouth and head that made her dizzy with the shock. She still refused, rejoicing in her heart that she had not revealed anything about the precious pages." So moves the story of a boy and a girl, committed Christians and deeply in love, during 24 years of separation and suffering. This personalized story of China's persecuted church will startle, grip and convict your heart as it has mine.

Edwin W Kilbourne, China Hand,
OMS International, Vice President-at-Large.

China's People's Republic of China (PRC), has the largest population in the world, 1.3 billion, one fifth of the world's population. With this staggering number of inhabitants, the urgent cry from

Introduction

China has attracted the renewed attention of Christian mission strategies including an exciting new book, Exiles of Hope. Enthusiastically I am delighted to endorse this book. This unique volume by Anthony Bollback describes the sufferings—and victories of fellow believers in China—with first hand experiences on the field. It continues the story of *Red Runs the River*, a popular bestseller.

Ben Armstrong, PhD
Former founding director, Trans World Radio
Executive director National Religious Broadcasters,
NRB, 1965-89

Chapter 1

THE SONG NEVER CEASED

Startled, Sister Sung awakened from a sound sleep, aware that God had spoken to her in a vivid dream. The Bible Woman of the Taiping Church was not accustomed to such dreams, but she knew instinctively that God was communicating something special to her.

In the dream she had seen three young women working in a rice field. As she watched, they gathered in a huddle and bowed their heads, as if in prayer. Then she seemed to hear a voice from heaven speaking to her saying: *"As soon as it is daylight, go to the north end of the commune farm, and there you will find three women. As you approach them, sing 'Onward, Christian Soldiers.'"*

She pondered the meaning of this dream and thought for a moment. *It would be very foolish in times like these to walk along the road singing a Christian song. These are very dangerous times to be singing aloud in broad daylight!*

"My child," the Lord continued speaking quietly to her heart, *"those three women need the comfort of My Word. Now go, and I will be with you."*

"*Lord Jesus,* she responded, "*even the rocks seem to have ears these days, but if You send me on this errand, I will do as You say.*"

Sleep eluded her for the rest of the night as she lay on her bed, praying for strength to carry out this unusual task. As dawn broke in the eastern sky, she arose and continued praying for God to lead her.

"What am I to do other than sing?" she prayed as she dressed to leave. A thought flashed through her mind. *"You will know what to do when you get there."*

Cautiously opening the door of her small apartment, she looked in both directions before stepping out. Tiptoeing down the hall, she made her way to the street, furtively glancing in all directions. One could never be sure who was watching. Someone was always ready to report any strange actions to the Communist Party representative of the area. After all, everyone was hungry these days, and rations were small. Useful reports to the authorities often brought extra rations, especially if they involved Christians. Desperate people stoop to anything for a morsel of food.

The town was just beginning to stir and only a few hawkers were around, calling out their breakfast treats for early-risers. She moved along quietly, assured that she was following her Lord's command. Reaching the north end of town, she proceeded along the edge of the rice field until she saw three women already at work in the field. They huddled together for a few moments, just as in her dream.

"Those are the women I am sending you to," she heard the Voice in her heart say. *"Sing as you approach them."*

She looked around once again. No one was in the area except the three women. Softly she began to sing as she approached them:

Onward, Christian soldiers, marching as to war,
With the cross of Jesus going on before.
Christ, the Royal Master, leads against the foe.
Forward into battle, see His banners go!

In the quietness of the morning, her song floated over the field. The three women were working in a huge commune field planting rice shoots, one after the other in orderly fashion. It was backbreaking work that would one day blossom into full heads of rice and a rich harvest, but it was no easy task for city girls unaccustomed to such labor.

Meiling's heart was heavy as she thought of the sad news her mother had sent in the annual letter permitted. The sad news was that her mother had been further humiliated by the authorities and ordered to become a street sweeper in Puyang! With more than half of her sentence still to be completed, she wondered how her mother could survive. Hot, scalding tears dropped into the mud, watering each plant she stuck in the ground.

"Oh, Lord," she cried softly, "how long must we bear this pain? My poor mother! Sweeping the streets! And, my father, suffering in the dark coal mines of Datung! And Anching! Is he dead or alive? How can I bear all this sorrow?"

It was just a few years ago that she had been the honored daughter of the most prestigious high school principal in the Puyang area. However, when the Communists had secured the area, Meiling's father soon became the object of their scorn. Brought up for trial, he was deposed as principal and sentenced to ten years in the northern coal mines of Datung. Things soon deteriorated for Meiling, too. After being expelled from the university for being the daughter of a convicted felon, she found a low-level job as a nurse's aid in the local hospital. She recalled with a shudder how the lecherous administrator had laid his lustful eyes on her and demanded that she become his mistress.

When Meiling persisted in resisting his advances and demands, he finally determined to make a public spectacle of her. He himself would administer the public beating! His first attempt failed when he was suddenly seized with a heart attack but, after recovering, he attempted the beating again. Once again, Meiling was spared as he died suddenly in a fit of rage. The new administrator and staff became fearful that somehow the man's death would come back to haunt them if Meiling remained on the job. They solved their problem by having her sent to a commune for five years of "reeducation." Life had turned sour at every turn for her. Now, on this day, she wept bitter tears of pain and discouragement.

It was at that moment that Sister Sung's song floated gently through the air. Meiling paused and looked around.

Singing! Someone is singing! *What is there to sing about?* she thought. Then it struck her: *I know that tune. Why that's "Onward, Christian Soldiers!" I haven't heard that hymn since I arrived at this commune! Who dares to sing that hymn out here?*

Following the sound, she noticed an elderly woman, stooped with age, slowly moving toward her. The words of the song were becoming clearer now. Her heart warmed to the words of victory:

> At the sign of triumph Satan's host doth flee,
> On, then, Christian soldiers! On to victory!
> Hell's foundations quiver at the shout of praise,
> Christians, lift your voices. Loud your anthems raise!

The elderly woman was moving slowly toward them, looking boldly at the three who stopped and stared. Then, with a surge of joy flooding her heart, Meiling dropped her plants and rushed to the woman.

"Sister, sister," she bubbled, excitedly. "You are a sister in the Lord! I know that song. I too am a believer."

The two women embraced as the tears coursed down Meiling's face.

"I was weeping tears of pain a few moments ago," she admitted, as she dried her tears on her sleeve, "and I asked my Lord how much longer must I endure this pain? Then I heard your voice. Oh, sister, thank you for that song in the night! But what are you doing here? It is so dangerous to sing a hymn in public?"

"Oh, my child," she said tenderly, still holding Meiling in her arms. "The Lord showed me in a dream that there were three women out here, and He told me to come out here singing 'Onward, Christian Soldiers,' because you needed to be encouraged in the Lord. So, here I am, an obedient child, just doing what He told me to do!"

"We three are Christians," Meiling replied happily, as the other two women joined her, "but we know of no one else who is. We are starved for the fellowship of other believers."

"I am Sister Sung, the Bible Woman from the Taiping Church," the elderly woman acknowledged. "The Lord sent me here to lift your spirits and to tell you where the believers meet. It is dangerous to meet together, but we must or we will shrivel up and die."

"You are right," replied Meiling, still clinging to the older woman. "I feel so dried up inside. I have been here in this commune for two years already. These two sisters have joined me in walking the pathway to heaven, but the only fellowship we have is with one another."

"Well, praise the Lord," replied Sister Sung happily. "The believers will be meeting tonight at 3 A.M. in order to avoid detection. Would you like to join the gathering?"

Without hesitation they made plans to meet two blocks south of the commune dormitory. Sister Sung moved on quickly as the girls returned to their work, but Meiling's heart was bursting with praise. God had heard her anguished cry and filled her heart to overflowing!

The three women crept stealthily out of their dormitory at different intervals and met at the appointed place. Sister Sung was already there, waiting expectantly.

"Follow me as quietly as possible," she admonished them. "We must not arouse suspicion or we will all suffer serious consequences."

They moved along in the shadows of the houses until they reached the designated home. Slipping quietly inside, Sister Sung introduced the three women to the people gathered for worship and explained how God had spoken to her in a dream. In the dim light, the faces of the ten people gathered could hardly be distinguished, but there was no mistaking the sincere words of welcome whispered around the circle. Joy swept over the three women as they listened to an unfamiliar but marvelous hymn of praise the people sang softly in little more than a whisper.

For Meiling's two young converts, this was the first time they had ever met with a group of Christians. Meiling's heart was flooded with precious memories of the days when she and Anching had worshipped in the Puyang Church and listened to Pastor Yang's inspiring messages.

Oh, how long ago that was! she thought. *Oh, how much sorrow we have suffered. How long, dear Jesus? How long must this go on?*

Sister Sung led the service and encouraged the believers as she explained a passage from the Bible. Meiling sensed the holy presence of God as the group sat huddled together, whispering their songs of praise and listening intently to the message of hope.

"Our dear pastor," said Sister Sung, "has not been heard from since he was arrested three months ago. We must uphold him and his family in prayer during this time of testing. Be strong in the Lord, dear brothers and sisters. He is Victor. Satan cannot overcome God's people, nor wipe out His church. Some day this awful night will be ended. Let us be faithful in the darkness and let our lights shine forth for our wonderful Lord and Savior, Jesus Christ."

By 4 A.M. the believers began to quietly leave, one or two at a time, in order to avoid detection. Meiling and her companions walked quickly back to their barracks, making certain to stay well hidden in the shadows of the buildings. Suddenly a vehicle turned a corner, bathing the street in headlight glare.

"Quick! Into the alley! Lie down among the rubbish and don't move," whispered Meiling urgently, as she shoved her friends to the ground. The police patrol slowly approached, as the officers searched the area. The car stopped at the alley entrance, and a policeman pointed his light into the shadows.

"It's OK," he said as he played his light up the alley and over the heaps of rubbish. "Nothing but garbage."

The car moved on as the trembling girls lay still for a few more moments.

"That was a close one," whispered Meiling with relief.

"We're not back in our rooms yet," reminded one of the girls. "I'm not sure I want to do this very often."

They reached their rooms unnoticed, exhilarated by the worship but terrified at the terrible price they would have had to pay if they had been discovered.

The words of Psalm 91 flashed into Meiling's mind as she lay trembling in her bed: "A thousand shall fall at your side, but it will not come near you" (Psalm 91:7).

"Thank You, precious Jesus," she breathed as she closed her eyes in sleep. *"Those few minutes of fellowship with other believers were worth it all!"*

Chapter 2

HONG KONG HEARTACHE

The defeat of the government troops by the overpowering Communists in 1949 started a long chain of unparalleled misery for millions of Chinese. Frantically fleeing southward, thousands died of starvation and disease and were buried in shallow graves or left beside the roads they were traveling. Anching and Wenpei had walked more than five hundred torturous miles to the Hong Kong border, escaping into the one tiny enclave of freedom on the South China mainland.

In late 1948 Anching had been torn away from his family (and Meiling) and sent north to the battlefront. He could never forget that tragic moment when his truck pulled away from his loved ones, nor could he forget the promise he had made to Meiling.

"I will find you again, no matter where you are—even if it takes the rest of my life," he remembered calling out to her. Now safely in Hong Kong, he wondered how he could ever keep that promise. Everywhere along the border bedlam prevailed. Weary, bedraggled refugees clamored for water and food.

"Help us," they cried. "Have pity on us. We're starving!" A terrible sense of loss and loneliness gripped Anching and Wenpei, who had fought together in the war. Now defeated, they had become refugees, and like so many others they were footsore and weary from the long trek. Food was scarce or non-existent, and hunger was always stalking them. Hiding during the day and traveling by night through areas occupied by Communist troops had taken its toll on the two men, physically and emotionally. Both were mere skin and bones.

"At least we made it to safety," Anching said wearily, as he slumped to the ground.

"True," Wenpei replied slowly, "but now what do we do? Where can we find food? Look at these masses crying out for help!"

"Our God has not deserted us," Anching replied, with a smile that lit up his gaunt face. "God preserved us that night when we were ducking flying bullets and mortar shells in that last battle, remember? And He will not desert us now."

Noticing a long line of shoving, shouting people forming nearby, Wenpei spoke to a man beside him.

"What's going on?"

"Its chow time," the man responded. "Quick, get into line for a bowl of rice."

Both men jumped at the word "food" and quickly joined the long line of hungry people impatiently pushing their way toward the steaming cauldrons of rice and vegetables being provided by the government. One large bowl of rice, topped with a few vegetables, could hardly satisfy their hunger after months of scrounging in garbage bins, but they liked the sound of the instructions being given.

"Come back tomorrow for more," shouted the harried relief workers, who ladled out the food as fast as they could.

"Eat it slowly," Anching advised. "Make every mouthful last as long as possible."

"I never realized how good a bowl of rice could taste!" commented Wenpei between mouthfuls.

Five long, wretched years had passed since Anching had been forced into the army truck at gunpoint in his hometown of Puyang, a suburb of the metropolis of Wuhan. Now that he had made it to a refugee camp on an isolated hillside called *Rennie's Mill* in Hong Kong, life was anything but luxurious. In fact, it was a constant struggle for survival and was almost as bleak as the long trek to Hong Kong had been. But there was some compensation for the spartan life, as the pair would soon discover.

It was here that they had met some missionaries, themselves evacuees from North China, who were moved with compassion for the destitute multitudes. Before long a church was started and eventually a Bible School. Anching and Wenpei were part of the first class and, along with the missionaries, had actively worked to bring order out of chaos. The student body had grown to more than two hundred, and although most were new believers since arriving in camp, they were all filled with a passion to reach others with the gospel of hope.

Although Anching had many friends his heart ached daily as he thought of Meiling somewhere back in China. Perhaps she was suffering unbelievable misery at the hands of the Communists. His one consolation was the certainty that her love for Jesus was so strong that nothing could shake her faith. He knew she would die for Jesus if necessary. Little did he realize the pain she was enduring at that very moment at the hands of the hospital administrator. All he could do was pray and hope that she was still alive, serving Jesus no matter what the cost. His promise, made more than five years ago, still burned in his heart.

In spite of his resolve, a complication had unexpectedly cropped up. It had been a year since Sumei, a vivacious young woman, had joined the student body. Her story, like all the others, was full of tragedy and sorrow. Her father had died in one of the battles some years before, and she and her mother had fled southward. The two women had trudged along day after day until, weak with exhaustion and starvation, her dear mother had finally lain down under a tree and never awakened. Alone and frightened, Sumei had enlisted some others nearby to help dig a shallow grave. Then she was forced to move on, until at last she had reached the safety of the refugee camp at Rennie's Mill.

Destitute and frightened, and not knowing where she could even sleep that night, she disembarked from the barge that had deposited another swarm of refugees on shore. She was immediately attracted by the sound of singing coming from a small group of young people. Filled with curiosity, she moved toward them, all the while wondering how anyone could sing in this sad world.

As she moved closer she was amazed to hear these young people singing and talking about a man named Jesus, who had changed their lives and had put a song back in their hearts. Transfixed, she listened attentively. When one of the young men invited anyone interested to step forward and talk to them about Jesus, she found herself irresistibly inching her way forward. Never in her life had she witnessed anything like the radiance that shown from the faces of these young people!

What in the world had changed them?

A couple of young women engaged her in conversation and shared with her the thrilling story of Jesus and salvation. Realizing that she had just landed, they asked if she had any friends or relatives in the camp.

"I'm all alone and I don't know anyone here," she confessed, as tears welled up in her pretty eyes.

"Then you must come with us to our school," they answered. "We will find some place for you to stay for a few days and get you settled," they assured her.

"Oh, thank you," she said, as the tears flowed freely down her cheeks. "It has been so long since anyone has been this kind to me," she sobbed. It wasn't many nights later, at the big tent meeting, that she prayed to receive Jesus into her life, and before long she was enrolled as the newest student in the school.

Pretty and vivacious, Sumei was soon fully involved in the life of the school and all of its activities. Before long she became a vital part of the witnessing team that Anching led. Three or four times a week his team led street meetings in various parts of the camp, and dozens of people embraced Christ at each meeting. Those were exciting days, as the church and school grew and its influence increased in the makeshift shantytown.

The problem for Anching was the attraction toward Sumei that was growing in his heart. She was so much like Meiling that at times he had to excuse himself and get alone to think. The struggle with his old promise to Meiling was taking on new significance. His mind raged with questions.

Was it a valid promise that I made in the emotions of the moment? Is there any possibility that I will ever be able to return to China and search for Meiling? Is she even alive? These thoughts tortured him day and night.

One day a small group of students was reminiscing about the earliest days of Rennie's Mill camp, and since Wenpei and Anching were two of the very first to arrive, they had many stories to share. Sumei listened with rapt attention, especially when Anching was speaking.

"We were transported by barge to this barren hillside," Anching began, "like all the refugees arriving in those days. At that time this was only a barren, rocky hillside with a few shrubs. The only structure here was the dilapidated noodle factory that now serves as Haven of Hope Hospital."

Wenpei jumped into the conversation.

"I remember the shock of seeing this place for the first time. Everyone on our barge exclaimed with disbelief, 'There's nothing here! Where are the homes we were promised?'

"The frustrated Hong Kong police officers were desperately trying to control the crowd," Anching continued.

"'Get in line,'" they ordered. "'You will be issued building materials and tools to build your own places,' an officer called out. 'The government is doing its best to help you, so get in line and pick up your supplies. Then stake out a spot anywhere you choose, but be sure it is not more than six feet by eight feet per person! Those who go beyond that limit will have their huts torn down. That's all we can do for now,' he said apologetically as he tried to placate the angry mob. The crowd surged forward, angrily shouting its displeasure. Out of necessity the small police contingent was forced to restore order by rushing forward with swinging batons."

"What happened then?" Sumei asked, looking straight into Anching's eyes. His heart skipped a beat as a strange feeling for her welled up in his heart!

Why is this happening to me? he asked himself. *I made a promise to Meiling, and I will keep it*, he determined, as he fought to control his emotions. Wenpei sensed Anching's struggle and rushed to the rescue.

"Oh, I can finish that story better than Anching," he said with a hearty laugh. "He'd never tell you the real facts, anyway. He's too humble for that."

Everyone chuckled, knowing how true that was.

"Well, you see, it was like this...." Wenpei continued. "Anching just spoke up in a clear voice and said to me, 'Let's pick up our supplies and find a spot to build. Come on, everyone, it's not all that hopeless. We're free, aren't we?' You should have seen the response in that crowd. The grumbling stopped as people lined up for their supplies. Well, you all know Anching. He's the one who always finds the right solution."

A chorus of agreement erupted, causing Anching further embarrassment. Sumei made a mental note of this remarkable man who attracted everyone's attention.

I'd like to know him better, she thought, *and I'd like to know the reason why all the girls like him so much but none claims him in any special way!*

"Go on," someone called out, interrupting Sumei's thoughts. "What happened next?"

A fellow student named Han spoke up.

"I was also on that first load of refugees with Anching and Wenpei. The three of us lived together in those days in a little shack we'd built. I wasn't a believer at the time, but watching these two under those circumstances soon convinced me that they had discovered something I really wanted. Soon after I became a believer, dysentery broke out in the camp and hundreds died from that dread disease. It was Anching and Wenpei who took leadership and devised a plan for building strategically located latrines. Work was progressing steadily and people were actually pitching in to get the job done. These two were growing in popularity as people recognized what they were attempting to do. With the first latrine up and operating near the police outpost, refugees redoubled their efforts to complete the one nearest to their huts.

"'You fellows have saved us from certain death,' one woman called out loudly as the two of them arrived to check on the work being done. 'We all say thank you for helping us,' she continued."

Han continued as every eye focused on him. "People nearby patted them on the shoulder and praised them for their efforts," he said, beaming at his two friends, "but standing at the back of the crowd was a man with an ugly scar on his face. Glaring menacingly at Anching, he called out, 'It would be a good idea if you guys left us alone in this area of the camp. I'm the *boss* here, and I don't tolerate any interference from outsiders, and especially from those who work for foreigners.' He tossed his head arrogantly as he looked around at the frightened people.

"Hearing this exchange," continued Han, "expressions changed on the faces of the people. They silently stole away, not daring to look at Anching and Wenpei. We talked about that fellow later when we returned to our shack.

"'I don't like the looks of that fellow,' Anching said to us. 'I think he's a troublemaker. We'd better watch out for him because I think trouble is brewing.' The three of us had the same feeling. I remember Wenpei saying he thought the man had an evil look in his eyes. My question was, 'What do you make of him saying he's the *boss* and doesn't like people who work for foreigners?'

"Anching's answer to that was, 'The only thing I can think of is that he's from one of the old triads in China, still intending to extort money or favors from the people living in what he calls his area.' We all agreed that he must be from one of those gangs, made up of roughnecks who were always ready to stir up trouble," continued Han, now thoroughly enjoying the limelight.

"Anching's mind was filled with great plans for improving the lot of the people and, with the help of the missionaries at the Bible School and the hospital, we were provided with some funds to get the latrines finished. At night we returned home, exhausted from the rigorous work of digging the deep holes."

Wenpei picked up the story at this point.

"One morning as Anching was making his rounds inspecting the sites where work on the latrines was in progress, he noticed a large crowd gathered around the site in the area where the *boss* operated.

"'Oh, Anching!' wailed a young mother with her baby strapped to her back. 'Come see what someone did during the night. They filled in the hole the men were digging yesterday!'

"'What?' he cried out in dismay. 'Someone actually filled in the hole during the night?' he asked incredulously. Sure enough he saw that the piles of dirt had been shoveled back into the hole. All of yesterday's work had been done for naught!

"'Who could have done this?' asked an angry man that had done a lot of the digging. 'Why would anyone do such a thing? This latrine is good for all of us. I can't understand this at all!'

"'Send someone to call the police.' Anching ordered. 'This is nothing less than sabotage! We must find the culprits and put a stop to it,' he said loudly for all to hear."

The girls leaned forward, hanging onto every word, as Wenpei continued.

"The police took charge immediately, but everyone professed to know nothing about the incident, and no one knew anything about a man with a scar. He simply was nowhere to be found, and no one was able to give any clues as to who he was. The police noticed that at the mention of the man everyone seemed to clam up.

"'I believe these people have been threatened,' the officer said to Anching.

"'I think you're right' Anching responded. 'This looks like the work of a gang that doesn't want any interference in its territory. It could be drugs or prostitution—almost anything—that motivates them, but it's definitely nothing good.'

"'These guys are dangerous, too,' continued the officer, 'so you'd better be careful. They'll stop at nothing.'

"Anching tried hard to persuade the men to return to digging," chimed in Han at this point. "Everyone just disappeared after making one lame excuse after another. The enthusiasm for the latrine project displayed the day before had now mysteriously evaporated. Baffled, we returned to our hut, wondering what our next step should be. In the morning we conferred with the missionary and asked for a couple of extra men to help us. Anching was confident that these two extra men would help get the hole dug out again by nightfall. As we approached the site, a young girl who had been attending the evening tent meetings walked by slowly. Nodding to Anching, she spoke softly, as she continued walking past him.

"'We've all been threatened by the *boss*,' she whispered. 'Everyone is afraid to come and help you. Please be careful. The *boss* has threatened to kill you,' she added fearfully, continuing on her way without stopping.'

"'Did you hear that?' Anching asked us. 'The *boss* is threatening to kill me!'"

Han continued the story, as everyone sat spellbound.

"'I think only two of us should go down into the hole,' Wenpei suggested, 'while the others move the earth back away from the hole and keep a sharp lookout for anything suspicious.'

"'That's a good suggestion,' Anching responded. 'I hate to ask you guys to work here with such threats. Maybe you'd better return to your regular jobs.'

"'And leave you here alone to do all the work? I protested. No way! We're sticking with you!'" Han added this last statement with a flourish, as everyone riveted their eyes on him.

"'OK,' Anching replied, 'but keep a sharp lookout for anything suspicious.'"

Wenpei picked up the story again.

"Some time passed as we worked to reopen the hole. Unexpectedly, a small child came running up to the edge of the hole, tossed a paper into the hole, and then turned and disappeared among the shacks. It floated down at Anching's feet. Picking it up, he quickly glanced at it, as a feeling of foreboding swept over him. The note said, 'If you value your life, stop the work. I'm in charge here, and I will not tolerate any interference from outsiders that work for foreigners.' Anching slowly passed the paper around to the rest of us as he spoke.

"'Well, the battle lines are definitely being drawn by the *boss*,' he said. 'Sounds like we're in for some serious trouble.' Late in the afternoon, Anching sent Han and the other two men back to discuss the situation with the pastor and alert the police as to what was happening.

"'Wenpei and I will keep on working until dark,' he said, 'and then we'll join you and see what the next steps should be.'

"Let me tell you…." Han spoke up at this point. "I didn't agree to that. I told Anching emphatically that we all should stay on and finish the job, but in the end he persuaded me to go talk with the pastor and alert the police. Well, we all understood Anching's passion for this project, and though we didn't want to leave him and Wenpei alone, we did think it was important to alert the police."

"After the other three had left," continued Anching, "Wenpei and I continued digging until dusk settled in. We both felt satisfied with the amount of work accomplished. The job was well on the way to completion. Well, as we were preparing to climb out of the deep hole, suddenly there was a shower of dirt falling in around us. I looked up just in time to see a large rock hurtling in my direction. As I jumped quickly aside, it just missed me. I began climbing out as quickly as possible, but dirt and rocks continued to pour in.

"*Could the sides be collapsing?* I wondered, as I clambered to the top. *Or is someone shoveling the dirt in?*

"Now the dirt was coming from all directions. A large stone glanced off my shoulder as I neared the top. *Good thing that didn't hit me on the head*, I thought. *I wonder how Wenpei is making out?* But there was no time to look back. Reaching the top I was shocked to see three masked men shoveling furiously.

"'Hey, stop that!' I yelled. Two of the men rushed me and attempted to push me back into the hole."

The girls who sat listening shuddered in horror, while every fellow around the table leaned forward so as not to miss a single word.

"'Oh, no you don't,' I shouted at the men," continued Anching. "Then I grabbed one of them nearest me and pulled him off the loose dirt at the top. The man began a fast slide toward the edge of the hole and plummeted to the bottom with a scream. Wenpei had scrambled out by that time, and we braced ourselves as the other two men rushed us."

"Let me finish this story," pleaded Wenpei, with excitement.

"I'll never forget that fight! It was fierce! We managed to move away from the hole as we shouted for help. Both of us used every trick of self defense we had learned in the army. Anching was good with his feet. You should have seen the blow that sent one of the fellows sprawling to the ground," said Wenpei, as he demonstrated a hard kick.

"Ah, it wasn't all that special, Wenpei. You're exaggerating!" Anching said, with a sheepish smile.

"I'm not exaggerating! It was a solid kick, my friend. I think that thug still remembers that blow!" said Wenpei, as everyone joined in laughter. "But those guys were big and strong," Wenpei continued, as the laughter died down.

"We were in a life and death struggle—and it wasn't over yet. I wondered how much longer we could hold out, as the fight see-sawed back and forth. I was knocked off my feet with a solid blow to my head. Those guys took advantage of the situation...and both of them jumped Anching. They caught him with a fierce blow that sent him reeling down the rough slope until he landed with a thud against the wall of a shack.

"He lay there stunned for a moment, unable to move. In seconds the two men pounced on him, pounding him blow after blow. One of the masked fighters picked up a bamboo pole lying nearby and began pummeling him. He covered his head with his arms as he tried to ward off the brutal attack. I scrambled to my feet and rushed to help him.

"Fortunately, the commotion brought people to the doors of their huts and a few brave men rushed out to stop the fight. Not wanting to be caught, the two men made a hasty retreat, as the third man was climbing painfully out of the hole. They all escaped into the darkness. Anching lay still as the people rushed to help him.

"'It's Anching,' wailed an older woman who frequently stopped to talk with him. 'Someone help me,' she cried. 'Bring me some water. He's bleeding!'

"I have to admit," Anching spoke up, "the two of us were a sorry-looking mess. I was sitting by the side of the hut, dazed from the beating, and Wenpei looked like a gangster with his eye swollen shut." He grinned, as the students sat spellbound.

"We had put up a good fight," Wenpei added, "but those thugs were too much for us.

"'Who did this?' the people standing around demanded. No one answered immediately. Then the older woman spoke up.

"'It's that wicked *boss*. This is his doing. That gang is trying to frighten us all into submission. Well, I for one will not give in,' she cried vehemently. 'We came here to find freedom from violent men, so let's stand up and fight these evil ones,' she continued defiantly. No one made any comment, but all went quietly about, trying to help the two of us. The older woman knelt by Anching's side, as she bathed his head gently and wiped the blood from his eyes.

"'Oh, you poor man,' she said sympathetically. 'They almost killed you! And to think they are trying to stop the good work you men are doing for all of us! They are beasts, and we'll fight them. Won't we?' she asked vehemently, as she paused a moment in caring for Anching's wounds. 'Won't we?' she asked again in a louder voice when no one responded.

"'It won't be as easy as you think,' a man volunteered. 'These thugs are nasty and will stop at nothing, but if we don't pull together, they'll take over this place and ruin our lives. Then it will be just as bad as what we left behind in China.'

"Anching opened his mouth to speak, but his lips were so swollen it was difficult to understand him.

"'We'll need the help of the police,' he said with difficulty, '...and God.' Darkness had settled in as the little group helped Anching to his feet. He wobbled a little as he tried to climb back up to the path."

"Wow! What an experience," echoed the students as they looked admiringly at the three men.

"Let me tell you," Han interjected, "these two looked terrible when the villagers brought them to the clinic. We got them patched up and into their bunks in our hut," Han added with a satisfied smile. "I stayed up most of the night with them," he remembered.

"Han was a terrific nurse," Anching added, as he looked over at their friend. "I don't know what we would have done without him."

What no one knew was that night sleep eluded Anching again, as on so many other lonely nights…when his thoughts and prayers drifted back to China and Meiling somewhere in that vast country. He struggled with his painful dilemma—his relationship with Sumei, who was here, and Meiling, who was somewhere in China—and could even be dead by now for all he knew!

When will I ever see her again? Anching thought to himself. *How can I be sure she is alive and waiting for me?* Maybe she has even forgotten about me, he thought, as he tossed in his bed. It was early morning when fatigue finally overtook him and he fell into a fitful sleep, only to be awakened from a frequently recurring dream of seeing Meiling suddenly appear out of nowhere. Rushing toward her in his dream, she would always disappear just as suddenly as she had appeared. Waking, he would find himself trembling all over as he realized it was another cruel dream.

It was at such times that he thought of Jesus standing in the small, tossing fishing boat on the Lake of Galilee as He commanded the turbulent wind and waves to be quiet. Breathing a prayer, he asked Jesus to calm the raging storm in his life.

Lord Jesus, he prayed, *I made a promise to Meiling long ago, and I intend to keep that promise for the rest of my life!*

Chapter 3

THE DEATH BLOW

In the weeks that followed their first foray out of the dormitory to the secret meeting place, Meiling and her two friends relived that wonderful night over and over again.

"It is too dangerous for us to slip out of the dorm at night," Meiling said to her friends one day when they discussed the possibility of attending another meeting.

"I think you're right," one of the girls responded. "I was petrified when one of the girls in my section stirred in her sleep as I stealthily entered the room. If we had been discovered, we would have been punished severely."

"That's true," replied Meiling, in all seriousness, "but the fellowship was so precious. Still, I think we ought not to attempt that again. Maybe Sister Sung will come out this way again. That's what I'm praying will happen."

Two days later, early in the morning as the girls looked up from their backbreaking work, they saw the familiar form of an old lady hobbling along the road towards them. What a time of rejoicing as they gathered around their friend! Fellowship in Christ does not only take place in church buildings, they were discovering. God's

Presence was just as real and powerful in the field as they stood together in a little huddle and sang softly.

"We cannot stop our work," Meiling said after a few minutes, "or we will not make our daily quota. These few minutes have given us new strength and the Scripture is just what we needed to lift our spirits," she said, as Sister Sung prepared to leave. She had encouraged them from Daniel chapter three, with the story of the three men threatened by death in the fiery furnace.

"Remember what the men said to the king?" she asked. "'If we are thrown into the blazing furnace, the God we serve is able to deliver us from your hand, O King. But even if He does not, we will not serve your gods or worship the image of gold you have set up' (Daniel 3:18).

"My dear daughters in the faith," she continued, "these are very difficult days for all of us, but our God is greater than the government or the police, and He will not forsake us—even in times of great trial and suffering. He will always make a way of escape for us."

"Amen," responded the three girls, "and now we must go back to work. Oh, please come again, Sister Sung. We need you so much!"

"I will come whenever possible, and we will pray for you that God will add to your number and bring many into His kingdom, in spite of everything Satan will do."

Another month passed before Sister Sung appeared unexpectedly again. The girls were working in a distant field and dared not leave their work. Realizing the situation, Sister Sung did not hesitate a moment, but rolled up her trousers and waded into the muck to be with the girls.

"Oh, good morning, Sister Sung," they greeted her, as she struggled in the slippery mud of the rice field.

"Here let us help you," they offered.

"Good morning, and peace to all of you in the precious Name of Jesus. Now give me some rice plants to hold so that my presence here will not look suspicious. Remember what Jesus said?" she chuckled. "'Be as wise as serpents and as harmless as doves' (Matthew 10:16). "I will follow along with you as you work and we will worship the Lord."

Looking around, she noticed that there were no other workers nearby.

"Let us sing softly a song we have been learning," she said. "It goes like this:

'Lord Jesus, we worship and adore You.
We sing your praises night and day.
It is hard to live the Christian life unless You give us strength.
We need You, O dear Jesus, to fight the battle for us,
And give us victory in Your all-powerful Name.'"

After two or three attempts the girls had the words and the tune in mind. With other words of encouragement from Sister Sung and prayer, almost forty-five minutes had quickly passed in worship.

"I must return," Sister Sung said finally. "I must not cause any suspicion among the workers. But I will come again whenever possible."

The three girls embraced their dear friend, who was risking her life to visit them.

"Pray for us," Sister Sung requested. "More and more people want to attend the secret meetings. We must be very careful, though, lest someone deceive us and pretend to be a follower of Jesus. If someone infiltrates our ranks and informs the police of our meetings, we would all suffer very much. But we will not stop—though all hell is sent to oppose us!" she said triumphantly.

The girls watched with admiration as Sister Sung hobbled back down the road to town.

"What a remarkable lady! And she is so dedicated to Jesus!" they exclaimed, gazing after her as she went.

"God is using her in an astounding way," said Meiling. "We must pray that the Lord will protect her until her work is finished."

Meiling's five-year term in the commune was coming to a close and she anticipated returning home to Puyang to be with her mother. News from her father in the Datung coal mines was never adequate to answer all her questions. The annual letter from her mother informed her only that he was well and living in victory through the power of Jesus.

Reading between the lines she knew that it pierced her mother's heart to think of her husband confined to the darkness of the coal mine where he suffered so much from the cold and dampness. She herself was not well, and her job as a street cleaner added only to her misery. Nevertheless, there were no complaints; only the song of victory in the dark night that had enveloped China. Above all there burned in her heart the hope that one day the long exile would be over and her family would be back together again.

Meiling was impatiently anticipating her release to return home, until one day she was called into the supervisor's office. Anxiety filled her heart as she entered the room and faced the stern-faced supervisor. She was a woman in her fifties, stern in appearance in order to keep the hundreds of girls under her command in line. Yet beneath the outward appearance of sternness there was the shadow of kindness that Meiling had seen on more than one occasion.

"Meiling," she began slowly, "your term here in this commune is coming to an end within a few months. I know that you are anticipating a return to your home," she said without looking

Meiling in the eye. Her heart wavered as she watched the woman. She listened with a sense of foreboding.

What bad news does she have for me? Will I be forbidden to go? she wondered.

"I have just received new orders concerning you," continued the woman. "Within two months you will have completed your time here, but this order states that you will need to remain in the town. You cannot return to Puyang."

The news hit her like a huge ocean wave breaking over her with such powerful force that she momentarily swayed as if she would faint.

"Not return to Puyang?" she asked in a whisper.

"I'm truly sorry, Meiling," responded the supervisor with a sincere look of sympathy on her face. "You have been an exemplary worker here and I have appreciated your attitude so much. It has helped many of the girls in this commune. They have told me you have been their source of strength and help when everything seemed hopeless for them. I don't understand what has changed so many of them, but I know you have been responsible, and I thank you for it," she said.

"I have tried my best to be a help to everyone," Meiling responded weakly, "but I have been looking forward to returning to my mother, who is so ill. What is the reason I must remain in this town?"

"The order does not give any explanation. It only says you will not be issued a travel permit to Puyang. You will be free to leave the commune, but you will be restricted to this town. Do you understand?" she asked softly.

Tears filled Meiling's eyes as she bowed her head and whispered, "Yes, I do." Then, after a moment of fighting back the deep anguish of her heart, she asked, "How long will I be restricted to this town?"

"There is no date affixed, which means that it is indefinite." Again the supervisor looked down at her hands as she added her final words. "But, in time, you may apply to the police for a travel permit-at least for a visit to your home. I think that is all for now," she added, indicating that the interview was over.

Meiling turned and left the room with a heavy heart.

Free from the commune, but still a prisoner in the town, she thought. *All the hopes of these five years are dashed to pieces. Oh, Lord Jesus,* she prayed, *why is this happening to me now?*

That night Sister Sung made one of her unscheduled visits to the commune. The supervisor had allowed her a good measure of freedom to mingle with the girls after hours when she saw how the girl's spirits were lifted by the visits.

"Jesus impressed on my heart to come and visit you," she said, as Meiling embraced her warmly. "Is there something wrong, my child?" she asked tenderly as Meiling's hot tears touched her cheek.

"There, there," she whispered, stroking her long hair. "Jesus knows when our hearts are breaking, and He cares for us. Tell me, what is troubling you," she said, as she looked into Meiling's pretty, tear-filled eyes. For the next hour they talked quietly about this unexpected news.

"You must come and live with me," Sister Sung stated emphatically. "God has His purpose, but it is never to hurt His beloved children; it is only to shower His love on them. And also, you will experience the grace of God in this hour when your heart is breaking. Let us look for God's purpose and see what He has planned. Remember, dear child, God always has wonderful surprises for those who trust Him. He has one for you, too."

"Oh, thank you, Sister Sung. Having you here tonight is surprise enough for me. I want to see my dear mother again, but to be with you is the next best thing. I know God has many lessons to teach me, and you are the best teacher anyone could have."

"Oh, dear child, you will never know how much you have encouraged my heart through these years. Without your love and prayers, I would have failed long before this," she added gently. "Now dry your tears, and look to Jesus. He will never forsake you."

Each time Sister Sung visited them at the commune she taught them more and more of the Bible, as well as new songs of praise passed on by traveling evangelists. Faithful believers who would not give up their hope in Jesus had written most of the songs of adoration and praise from some foul prison cell. These were songs that captured the deep emotions of men and women who believed that Jesus is Victor and believed that, through Him, they too could be more than conquerors.

One morning another sister made her way out to the field, and in an agitated voice described the terrible scene that had occurred the night before in town.

"Fifteen people gathered at Elder Chu's home," she began, speaking between sobs. "Sister Sung was leading the singing, when suddenly there was a terrific pounding on the door and rough voices were demanding that the door be opened. Elder Chu opened the door immediately and eight or nine police officers rushed in, demanding to know who was the leader.

"Elder Chu stepped forward and explained politely that this was his home and these friends had come to visit with him. The captain slapped him hard across the face and spoke angrily.

"'This is an illegal Christian meeting that is forbidden,' he said. A couple of men rushed up to Sister Sung and grabbed her and shoved her toward the door. They said she was under arrest for breaking the law."

"Oh," gasped Meiling, "is she all right?"

"We haven't heard anything from her and the others who were arrested," the woman replied, as she dabbed her eyes. "Oh, Meiling, it was awful!"

"Was Elder Chu arrested also?"

"Meiling, that was the worst part. He was not arrested, but some of the police officers threw him against the wall and stretched his arms out, and then they nailed him to it!" she wailed.

"They nailed Elder Chu to the wall?" gasped Meiling and the other girls.

"The captain said, as he ordered him nailed to the wall, 'If you're going to follow this Jesus, then you will need to be crucified just like Him!' The people screamed at the police to stop, but they wouldn't listen. They just nailed him to the wall with two big spikes!"

"Didn't they arrest you?" Meiling asked.

"When the police rushed in, a couple of us were able to escape in the commotion. After the police vans pulled away, we crept back to the house. It was empty, except for Elder Chu.

"'Help me, sisters,' he pleaded. 'Get someone to take out these spikes,' he groaned.

"I ran to a believer's home and told them what had happened. Several men rushed over to Elder Chu's home to help him. It was awful! He was covered with blood and almost fainting from the pain. Oh. Meiling, it was awful. Elder Chu cried with pain as the men worked to free him."

"Oh, how cruel," cried Meiling, in horror. "And how is he now?"

"His hands are throbbing with pain, but he keeps telling everyone who comes to see him how glad he is that he could suffer in this way for Jesus. Several of the neighbors were shocked by what happened, but were so impressed with Elder Chu's response to his suffering that they prayed with him this morning to accept Jesus. He said the pain was worth it in order to see people coming to Jesus. Oh, Meiling, he has been such a witness to all of us!"

"Praise the Lord for Elder Chu and his faith," the girls repeated over and over again. "But what of Sister Sung and the others?" they asked anxiously.

"There is no word from them. We have been praying that they would be strong in the Lord and enabled by God to stand whatever pain is inflicted on them."

Meiling prayed softly as tears rolled down her face.

"Lord, watch over dear Sister Sung and the others as they are being interrogated and perhaps beaten. Help them to be bold in their witness for You, and heal Elder Chu's hands. Cause this terrible experience to lead many to You. In Jesus' Name. Amen."

"Amen," echoed the others softly as they wiped their tears.

"Now I must return quickly," the woman said, preparing to leave. "Someone will get a message to you as soon as we hear anything. We are praying for you, too. Be strong in the Lord," she said, as she started hastily back into town.

The girls resumed their work with heavy hearts but continued praying throughout the remainder of the day. Meiling was especially burdened for her dear friend, Sister Sung.

"Oh, God," she prayed, *"help your child to endure the suffering she must face and deliver her from the hatred of man."*

Little did she realize what was happening at the police station.

Standing before the police chief, elderly Sister Sung shifted from foot to foot in an attempt to relieve the pain. She had been standing there for more than an hour as the officer plied her with one question after another. He shrieked at her and warned her of the serious consequences for hiding any information to his questions.

"Tell me the names of the believers in this town," he shouted.

"I cannot do that," Sister Sung replied, with a quiet dignity not in evidence anywhere else in the room. Her peaceful demeanor seemed to threaten the chief, and he rose to shout into her face and demand the answers to his questions. Losing his patience, he struck her twice across her mouth, drawing blood from her lips.

"Answer me," he shouted. "If you refuse, we have ways to extract any information we want from you. Do you understand what I mean?" he asked menacingly, as he slapped her again.

"I am an old lady," she replied quietly. "You can hurt my old body, but you can never touch my soul, and you will never be able to pull Jesus out of my heart."

Furious at her response, the police chief ordered a bamboo pole to be brought. Holding it close to her face, he waved it angrily as he continued making demands for the names of all the believers. When he was unsuccessful, he raised his arm and struck her with a vicious blow across her back. The old lady crumpled to the floor as tears rolled from her eyes. As she fell, a small New Testament popped out of her jacket. It landed a few feet from her. She instinctively grabbed for her precious book.

"Oh, no you don't," he shouted as she reached for her book. With his boot, he stamped on her hand, causing her to cry out in pain.

"Is that a forbidden Bible?" he cried out in fury. "Let me see it," he ordered, as one of the police officers bent over to pick it up. Taking it in his hands, he opened it and read a few words. Screaming at Sister Sung, who was lying on the floor holding her bleeding hand, he shouted.

"You have been warned not to read this book, but you have disobeyed our great leader, Mao Zedong. You will be punished severely for this crime," he continued ranting. Holding the book high above his head, he cursed and threw it to the floor, right within reach of Sister Sung.

"Don't touch it," he yelled, as she reached to retrieve it. Raising his foot again, he crushed her other hand. Then, with great fury, he stamped on the New Testament again and again and ground his foot into it until its pages were torn apart. Finally, with much disdain, he spat on it, and on Sister Sung.

"Vermin," he screamed. "Our country will be better off without you Christians! We will wipe you out and destroy every vestige of Christianity in our land. We will bury the thought of this Jesus until every believer has returned to our great leader."

Looking at Sister Sung, who was weeping softly on the floor, he picked up his pole again and beat her unmercifully, stamping on her hands until they became a broken mass of raw flesh.

"There! That will teach you that disobeying our orders will bring swift punishment," he said.

With feeble voice, Sister Sung looked up at him and spoke weakly.

"Dear brother, I forgive you."

Enraged, the chief stomped on her head again and again, until she lost consciousness and lay in a crumpled heap on the floor. She never regained consciousness but passed into the Presence of her Lord. The angels and all heaven rejoiced as they welcomed her at the portals of heaven, shouting that another pilgrim had made it safely home!

Cautiously, the believers sent a message to Meiling and told her the full details of Sister Sung's death.

"Oh, Meiling," they cried, "she was an angel among us. She loved us so much and taught us God's Word. How will we survive without her? The police also searched Elder Chu's home from top to bottom and found his Bible. They confiscated it, along with some Christian literature they found there.

"From now on it will become even more difficult to gather for worship, but we will not stop spreading the good news," they asserted triumphantly.

The believers of the Taiping Church were overcome with grief as the news spread about Sister Sung's untimely death. It was like snatching away the closest member of every family to lose her. Elder Chu spoke quietly to each one as they came to weep.

"God has not forsaken us," he said over and over again as he raised his bandaged hands to bless them. "He has called our sister home. Her work was finished here. She is now forever in His Presence. We all know that 'to be absent from the body is to be present with the Lord,' (2 Corinthians 5:6) so don't feel sorry for Sister Sung. She is now exceedingly happy in the Presence of Jesus, and she would want us to be faithful until death. Look up. Let's see what God will do in these difficult circumstances."

The urgent problem was her burial. They dared not hold a public service, but neither could the police prevent a large crowd from gathering at the cemetery. Believers and non-believers alike loved Sister Sung, and many came to pay their last respects. As the coffin was lowered into the grave everyone just stood in silence, praying silently in their hearts. A large contingent of police officers stood at a distance, observing the proceedings and prepared to take whatever action was necessary.

Elder Chu braved the danger of arrest as he urged each one to be faithful to Jesus. He could not say all that was in his heart, but the sight of his bandaged hands spoke eloquently to everyone. Those hands said, "I am serving Jesus to the very end." In a few minutes the grave was closed and the people walked slowly back to their homes with a song in their hearts. One of God's precious children had been welcomed home. Elder Chu did encourage them to pray silently, to recommit their lives to Jesus, and then just to go on serving Him regardless of the consequences.

"That's what Sister Sung would want us to do," he encouraged, as those in attendance moved away from the grave.

A few weeks after Sister Sung's death, Meiling was released from the commune. Making her way into town, she wondered what was in store for her. Oh, how she had looked forward to living with Sister Sung and the opportunity of learning more about God's Word from her!

"Lord," she prayed silently as she walked into town, *"guide me and reveal to me your plan for my life and what I should do here in this town."*

A sweet sense of God's Presence flooded her heart, and it was as if she was hearing Sister Sung say, "Meiling, God has a wonderful surprise in store for you. Just follow Him."

As she walked along the Lord impressed on her to go to Elder Chu's home and seek his advice and help. When Mrs. Chu responded to the knock, she broke into a beautiful smile of joy and excitement.

"Oh, come in, Meiling. My husband and I were just praying for you and wondering when you would be released. Sister Sung told us you would not be permitted to return to Puyang. That certainly must be a terrible disappointment to you, but we must remember that God always uses our hurts to bless people and to strengthen us." Calling her husband, she said, "Come, see the visitor whom God has sent us today!"

"I already know who's here," he called joyously from the other room, where he had been resting.

"Ah, my dear Meiling," he said, coming into the room. "I just had a feeling that you would be coming to see us today! And are you free from responsibility at the commune?" he asked.

"Yes, Elder Chu, I have been granted the freedom to live in town and find some work here, but I cannot get a travel permit to return to my mother in Puyang. That hurts me so deeply because we have both waited so long for this moment. But, as Sister Sung used to say to me, 'God always has a place prepared for His children to serve Him.' I am just waiting for Him to reveal His will to me. I will follow Him wherever He leads me."

"That's wonderful! Mrs. Chu and I have been praying for you and for your future. How would you like to take over Sister Sung's responsibilities and be our Bible Woman?" he asked, with a beaming smile that did nothing to hide his emotions.

"Take Sister Sung's place?" she asked incredulously. "There is no way I could ever do that. Why, I don't know very much about the Bible and I have had no training. Besides, I am too young for such a position."

"Sister Sung has spoken to us many times about her hope that one day you would come to live with her and eventually take her place. She said she had never met anyone who was better prepared than you. Oh, Meiling, we are asking you to take up the unfinished task that dear Sister Sung left behind. She planned it all long ago, as if she knew her time here was very short. She wanted you to have her home and possessions, for she had no relatives."

Meiling looked at them, unable to speak, but with doubt visible on her young face.

"Meiling, will you accept this calling from God, even though it spells danger every minute—and possibly death and suffering?" Holding up his hands with the scars clearly visible, Elder Chu continued, "There is nothing better than to give your life to Jesus and to follow Him, no matter what the cost may be."

Overwhelmed, Meiling sat on the edge of her chair and stared in unbelief at the Elder and his wife.

"As I was walking into town, not knowing what I should do, I prayed that very prayer," she said with deep emotion. "I told

Jesus I would follow Him wherever He led me. But I am so weak, so unprepared. And I know so little of God's Word!"

"But you love Him with a passion. We have heard of your work among the women in the commune, and how many have followed Jesus. Whenever we are willing to obey God and allow Him to fill us with His Spirit, He does the rest. You will be one of the finest Bible Women we have ever had!"

Elder Chu continued sincerely. "Meiling, God is knocking on your heart's door. He needs you here, and He has many wonderful surprises in store for you."

Elder Chu talked on for a long time explaining what he envisioned for her to do, and then he prayed for God to demonstrate His mighty power through His young servant. Meiling wiped the tears from her eyes as he finished praying, knowing that she was experiencing one of those special God moments in her life.

Chapter 4

THE EYE OF THE STORM

The experiences you fellows had in the early days of Rennie's Mill Camp are very interesting," several students said one day, as they gathered around a table in the dining room.

"We've been wondering what happened after you were beaten up by those thugs, Anching?"

Sumei and her friends were quick to sit down with the group when they heard that remark.

"We want to hear the rest of that story, too," they said, joining the group of listeners.

"It is a story worth hearing," Wenpei responded with enthusiasm, especially since it revolves around our good friend, Anching. He was the hero in those days, and I can tell you—he is here only by the grace of God."

"Really?" several asked in surprise. "Come on, Anching, tell us the story!"

"No, I think I'd better tell the story," interrupted Wenpei. "He wouldn't tell you all the exciting stuff."

"Now you be careful, Wenpei, and don't add to the story just to make it more exciting," Anching cautioned with a quick laugh. "We don't want anyone thinking we can walk on water, you know!"

"Absolutely not," he replied with a twinkle in his eyes, "but some amazing and even dangerous things really did happen. Well, let's see. The other day we got as far as the part where we were beaten up badly by those thugs."

"Right," Sumei interjected. "Then what happened? I've been wondering ever since then how the story ended."

"Well, it's far from ended," Wenpei said, as he held back tantalizingly from rushing into the story. "All of this took place during our first year here, and that was six or seven years ago already." Everyone had grown very quiet as they waited patiently for him to continue.

"Anching made a slow recovery from the beating he took, and finally, after about ten days, he made another tour of the latrine sites. Some of the latrines were actually completed by that time and already in use. Approaching the site where the beating had taken place, several older women greeted him warmly as he passed by.

"'Oh, we're so glad you're still alive,' one woman said, as she continued scrubbing her laundry in a tub. Another spoke up, 'But you'd better be careful. Those evil men are not far away and they are determined to keep you or the police from interfering with their project.'"

"'Thanks,' he answered, 'but we can't let them take over this camp. I promise you I'll get the job finished somehow,' he replied, as he continued walking past her."

"Anching, I think you should tell the next part...about the woman and the baby," said Wenpei, turning toward his friend. Now every eye was riveted on him as he picked up the story from that point.

"Well, I had finished inspecting the area and found that the latrine had been filled in a second time. It made me angry to think that those evil men would risk the health of all the people of the camp for their own evil purposes. Just as I was preparing to return, a skinny woman with a baby in her arms called out to me very softly.

"'Please, help me!' she begged. 'My husband told me this morning that he is going to sell my little girl. We have no money to buy food for her,' she cried, bursting into tears. I looked at her scrawny, outstretched arms and knew that she was at the point of starvation. She thrust the little child towards me and begged me to take her.

"'Here!' she cried, 'Please take my child and protect her. My husband will sell her soon!'"

Sumei gasped with shock. "What did you do?" she asked, turning to look at Anching.

Wenpei could contain himself no longer but jumped in to continue the story. "I'll tell you what happened," he said. "Anching became very angry and replied, 'Sell your child? To whom?'

"'You know him,' the mother sobbed. 'The *boss*! The word is out that he is willing to pay one hundred dollars for a little girl. My husband is so desperate to provide for our family that he has finally succumbed to the offer,' she said weeping. 'Oh, please, save her!'"

Wenpei paused and, looking around at the other students, continued speaking. "For once our hero was speechless. When he recovered from the shock of this question, he asked, 'But what can I do with your child? How can I take care of her?'

"'But you must!' cried the mother. 'Oh, please, save my child from a life of brutal slavery. These wicked men are preying on poor people, who have no way to feed their children. They sell little girls to a ring of slave traders. Several children have already been sold to them. Oh, you must help me,' she pleaded. 'Take her to the missionaries,' she sobbed. 'They are good people. They will take care of her.'

"'And what about your husband?' Anching asked. 'What will he do when he finds out you have given your child to the missionaries?'

"'Believe me, he loves the child. He does not want to do this, but he has no other way. We have three other children. There are too many mouths to feed and there is so little food....'

"At that moment," continued Wenpei, she looked past Anching and exclaimed hysterically, 'Oh, here he comes now!'"

"Oh, Anching," Sumei cried with a shudder, "did you take another beating?"

"Not this time," he answered, "but I did brace myself to meet the unexpected."

"'What are you doing here?' the man who was coming towards us demanded sourly. I shot a swift prayer up to God for wisdom and courage.

"'Sir,' I answered, 'your wife has been pleading with me to help save your daughter.'

"'What can you do?' he replied, dejectedly. 'Your main interest is in building latrines. What about food? My family is starving! We have nothing to eat—and no way to work and earn money to buy food,' he replied bitterly. 'We need food more than a latrine!'

"His remarks felt like a swarm of bees had attacked me. I didn't have any answers for him, but I said, 'Come with me and I'll get you some food for tonight. I'll do my best to help you, but I am also a refugee and have no money. My friends at the medical tent will surely think of some way to help you.'

"'It's too late,' the man said, sorrowfully. 'I have agreed to sell the child tonight to get food for the others. There is no other way.' With that, he sat down and buried his face in his hands.

"'No,' I responded, 'please don't even think of selling the child. Let me try and help you. Come with me to the medical tent. I'm sure I can get some food for you.'

"'It's not just today,'" the man said. "What will we do tomorrow?" he asked, as his voice choked up.

"'Let's do something right now for your family,' I replied, 'before it is too late.

"'It's already too late,' the man repeated. 'I have already agreed to sell the child for one hundred dollars—*tonight!*'

"'Listen to Anching,' the mother pleaded. 'You know he's been trying to help us. You know he was beaten the other night just for us! Oh, please, go with him, and please, please don't sell our child!'"

"The man looked at his wife with desperation etched on his face as he replied. 'You know I don't want to sell the child, but what else can I do?'

"'Take her to the missionaries. Maybe they can help us,' she pleaded.

"'But I've already promised to deliver the child tonight after dark,' he replied, with the hopeless look of a desperate man. 'Who knows what they will do to us if we back out now?'

"I responded quickly when I heard that. 'Bring the child and let's go down immediately. We'll figure something out. Better bring your whole family. That will be the safest thing to do. We've got to find a way to help you,' I said, but in my heart I was shaking, wondering what I had gotten myself into."

The tension was suddenly broken as everyone burst into laughter.

"Knowing you," one of them said, "I'm sure some plan was already forming in your mind."

"Not really," I replied, "but I was sure the missionaries would find some way to help."

"I was in the medical tent when Anching came in," Wenpei said, with a hearty laugh. "He looked like a mother duck with her ducklings following behind. I remember saying to him, 'What's up, Anching? It looks like you've seen a ghost. You're as white as a sheet! Is something wrong?'

"'You'd better believe there's something wrong,' he replied. 'Not only wrong, but terribly dangerous.'"

"The missionary listened attentively to the whole story," added Han, who now took over the story.

"'Food for tonight isn't the problem,' the missionary replied, 'but those gang members will certainly cause us all a lot of trouble. But let's get this family some food right away. These little children are starving.'

It wasn't long before the missionary's wife had some food set before the hungry family. What a sight to see those little children eating their first real meal in who-knows-how-long. The grateful mother wept with gratitude as she watched the children eating. As she daubed at her tears, she spoke.

"'The problem is that we have too many mouths to feed. Thank you for this meal, but what can we do about tomorrow?'"

Only the sound of children eating could be heard. *Yes, what about tomorrow? And what about the little girl who was to be sold tonight,* all the students wondered.

"Yes, hurry and tell us what happened to the baby girl?" several said anxiously.

"Several of us went back to the family hut," Wenpei continued, "and brought back some of their belongings. The parents smiled with relief as plans were made for them to spend the night in the medical tent.

"'How can we ever thank you?' they kept saying. 'We've heard that you Christians are kind. Now we know that for a fact. Oh, we are so grateful!'

"Anching asked them if they had ever attended the evening service. 'No, we haven't,' the father replied sheepishly. 'However, a couple of our neighbors have, and they said that it was really helpful to them. They invited us to attend, but we haven't done so yet, but we will tonight,' he said with a happy smile.

"As the service started, a seedy-looking character slipped into the back seat of the tent and sat slouched over through most of the service. I remember Anching saying that he wondered if that man had anything to do with the intended sale of that baby.

"'Hopefully, he is not connected with the *boss*,' I commented, 'but I have a strange feeling that he does have something to do with that gang.' Early the next day the father returned to his hut to collect some more items of clothing for his family. He was just about ready to leave when the door suddenly burst open. He came face to face with one of the masked gang members."

"Then what happened? Quick, tell us!" the group pleaded.

Wenpei was enjoying himself and slowly continued the story.

"The masked man spoke softly, but with an obviously threatening tone in his voice, as he demanded, 'What happened last night? You didn't show up. The *boss* doesn't like being stood up, you know. Something usually happens that people regret when they don't keep their promises to him. Do I make myself clear?' He paused for emphasis before adding, 'so, can we expect the completion of the deal tonight?'

"Trembling with fear, the father responded, 'I'm sorry, but I've changed my mind. I cannot go through with the arrangements. Please, leave us alone. We're just poor refugees.'

"'You made the arrangement with the *boss*, didn't you?' the man sneered. 'I advise you to keep it, or you'll suffer the consequences! And if you go to the police, it will be doubly hard for you. Understand?'

"Without waiting for an answer, the thug slipped out the door and disappeared among the huts. A while later Anching met the shaken father at the medical tent.

"'What will they do to us?' asked the distraught father. 'Maybe I'd better keep the arrangement tonight to protect the rest of my family,' he said in despair. 'But if I do, it will kill my poor wife.'

"'I think it is always better to do the right thing,' Anching responded, 'and to ask God for His help. I can't say what will happen, but God has never let me down. I believe He will help you, too, if you trust Him.'

"There was a long moment's pause as the father considered the situation.

"'I know it is wrong to sell my daughter into a life of slavery and abuse,' he finally answered. 'I will trust your God and do the right thing. I'll take whatever comes then with a clear conscience.'

"'Good,' Anching replied. 'Now, let's see if there is any land available in this vicinity where we can build you a hut.'"

"What an amazing story!" one of the girls said, twisting her handkerchief nervously in her hands. "What happened after that?"

Anching picked up the story again.

"Early the next morning an agitated neighbor of the family rushed into the medical tent with some shocking news.

"'Last night about midnight,' he began, trying to catch his breath, 'we were all awakened by the sound of loud banging. I rushed out to see what was causing it and, to my amazement, there were seven or eight masked men tearing down your hut,' he related to the shocked father.

"'There's nothing left standing!' he said, with fear punctuating every word. 'They've completely destroyed your hut!'

"'I was shocked at first,' said Anching, 'but then I recovered and spoke.

"'It was the gang all right. That's the way it operates. They aim to strike fear into everyone's heart so that they will give in to their demands.' The child's mother sat dumbfounded, clutching her daughter close to her breast.

"'What will they do next?' she asked anxiously."

"Pastor Sung joined us at that moment," Wenpei continued. 'I believe the *boss* is not a refugee like the rest of us. He has too much money and too much power to be one of us. He must be from a gang in Kowloon that has lots of connections to the slave trade in Southeast Asia. Young girls are worth a fortune, I hear.'

"'But what will stop them from pursuing my family?' asked the anxious father. 'How can I protect them from such evil people?'

"'We are helpless to do anything in our own strength,' replied Pastor Sung. 'But I believe the Lord will make a way and give all of us the protection we need. Let's cast ourselves on the Lord and let Him solve this problem. We are His children and this is His church, so I believe He will take care of all of us somehow.'

"'But what will the *boss* do next?' the man asked, as we all grappled with the problem.

"'Maybe the best answer to that question,' the pastor responded, 'is what will God do next? I think we'll all be surprised with God's answer to this challenge!'

"Well, that's enough for tonight," said Anching, with a deep yawn. "Let's save the rest of the story for another time."

"No, no! Go on," a chorus of voices called out. "What happened to the family?"

"I'll finish the story," Wenpei replied to the eager students.

"We got the family settled in a new shack in our part of the camp, hoping that they would be safe there. Well, one night Anching wanted to stop by and see how they were doing, but I was so tired I returned to our shack. 'Hurry home,' I said to him, as he started off to visit the family."

"'I'll be there soon,' he reassured me. 'I just want to see how they're doing. A couple of their children have come down with bad colds. Maybe they need some help or something.' But as he neared the home, several men jumped out of the darkness and knocked him to the ground. They began to pound him viciously, and although he was scoring some good blows, he was badly outnumbered by that gang."

"'What's going on?' someone shouted in the darkness, as doors began to open at the loud commotion going on. Realizing that people would soon be surrounding them, one of the men pulled out his knife and stabbed Anching repeatedly.'"

"Oh, no," the girls exclaimed all at once, leaning forward to catch every word of the story. Looking at Anching, Sumei spoke for everyone present.

"None of us ever realized how dangerous it was right here in Rennie's Mill! Go on, Wenpei, finish the story."

"Forgive me, Anching," Wenpei said, with an amused smile on his face as he noticed his friend's embarrassment. "But you know I'm not embellishing the story one bit!"

"Come on, Wenpei, finish the story," several students said, as they leaned forward to catch every word.

"Well, OK then. After the stabbing, Anching just lay there in a heap, blood pouring from his neck and shoulder. The neighborhood men rushed to his aid and picked him up and carried him to the medical tent. The doctor rushed in and saw Anching lying on a bench.

"'Anching, what happened? Who stabbed you?' he urgently questioned, but Anching was unconscious. 'Call in the Air Vac helicopter!' the doctor ordered.

"Twenty minutes later the helicopter hovered over the camp, searching for a landing spot.

"'He's been stabbed badly,' the doctor told the medics. 'Get him to the hospital as quickly as possible. His life is hanging by a thread.'"

"In less than five minutes the helicopter was airborne again. I remember Pastor Sung leading us in prayer as the helicopter took off," Wenpei continued. "It was a scary night for all of us as we realized that Satan was doing everything possible to stop God's work.

We all knew we were in a spiritual battle of huge proportions, and everyone prayed for God's protection against Satan's attacks, and for the Holy Spirit to spare Anching's life.

"In the morning the police found a can of gasoline that the men abandoned when the neighbors came to Anching's rescue.

"'They intended to set the home of the family with the baby on fire as revenge for changing their minds about selling the child,' an officer said. 'Anching surprised them and he suffered the consequences.'"

"For two days his life hung in the balance between life and death," Wenpei continued, "while we pleaded with God to spare him. I was by his side on the second afternoon, when his eyelids flickered open for the first time since the attack. He looked around dazed and asked what had happened.

"'You were stabbed twelve times,' I informed him, 'by some men who evidently intended to burn the home of the family with the baby. Pastor Sung said the best thing we could do was to pray that God would bring these criminals to justice and bring the slave trade to a close.'"

"So what did God do?" the listeners demanded. "We know Anching recovered," Sumei said, as she looked over at him with renewed interest and respect.

"But what about the criminals?" asked another girl.

"You may think I'm making this up," Wenpei continued, "but this is the truth. A few weeks later a really bad typhoon hit Hong Kong and Rennie's Mill Camp. It was a miserable, unforgettable night! Many shacks were completely demolished by the devastating wind. All people could do was huddle together in the open rain and hope for the coming of dawn. As morning finally came, the wind and rain subsided. We stood speechless as we surveyed the havoc left by the storm. People were battered and bruised from the collapse of their huts or from flying debris but, miraculously, no one in the area had been killed. As the all-clear bell rang, the homeless slipped and slid down the mountainside to the old noodle factory. One end had totally caved in. Only broken splinters of wood remained, but fortunately the clinic section was still standing. Every home had been affected in some way.

"Just then, loud shouting came from the direction of the area controlled by the *boss*. 'What's all that shouting about?' I asked in alarm.

"'I don't know,' Anching replied, 'but I think we'd better get over there as quickly as possible and see what's the matter.' Reaching the scene of the commotion, we were shocked to see a man lying face-down on the ground with a broken piece of lumber protruding hideously from his back!

"'Who is he?' Anching asked as he rushed up to the man."

"'He's the *boss*,' a man standing nearby offered, showing no emotion.

"'The *boss*?' Anching exclaimed in surprise. 'Was he here last night? I'd heard that he never stayed overnight.'

"'He waited too long to leave, and when he decided to go the waves were too high to board the launch. Several other gang members were injured, but he's the only one who was killed. The force of the wind drove that two-by-four right through his back!'

"'Well, maybe that will be the end of the gang here," said another man who stood nearby. 'I think we'll be able to get that latrine finished now without any further trouble. We're going to take back our community and make it like the other areas,' said the man vehemently. 'What this man did to us was threaten us with our lives unless we obeyed his commands. He's dead now, and we're free!'

"The shouts of the people left no doubt where their loyalties lay. As the police arrived, the crowd no longer was afraid to point out the men who had harassed them. They were quickly rounded up, as the villagers recounted the atrocities that the *boss* and his gang had inflicted on them.

"The little old woman who had cared for me the night of the beating," continued Anching, "spoke up, also.

"'Anching, you and the rest of the Christians are welcome in this area. We all must admit that your God did something spectacular in this camp. After all, only gang members were injured—and the *boss* was the only person who died! Now that's a miracle I would not believe unless I had seen it with my own eyes.'

"As Wenpei, Han, and I walked back to our badly damaged hut, Wenpei turned to me and said, 'Well, isn't that what you prayed for? You asked God to do something so everyone would know He had protected us in the storm. Well, He certainly did that, and He brought judgment on the one man who was causing all the trouble around here.'

"My response to that was, 'He sure did! And I have an idea it will cause many people to recognize that God did something very unusual here last night.'"

"That's an amazing story," several students said, all speaking up at once.

"I'm glad you told us this story, Wenpei," Sumei said, as she looked admiringly at the three men. "You fellows certainly have had some unusual experiences, and God has used you to touch many lives. My prediction is that we haven't heard the last of you fellows!" she said with a twinkle in her eyes.

A chorus of voices echoed the same sentiment.

The struggle in Anching's heart continued. Each night as he looked at Meiling's faded picture his heart sank, realizing the hopelessness of the situation. Reports of atrocities against Christians in China continued unabated, and the death toll seemed always to be rising.

It was a well-substantiated report that thousands of Christians were losing their lives under the relentless pressure of the Communist regime. The prospect of ever finding Meiling again grew increasingly hard to cling to. Some days Anching's heart felt as if it would break, but still he clung to the hope that she was alive. Nevertheless, the futility of the situation crushed him and made life itself seem almost unbearable.

Perhaps the dream of being reunited with Meiling again some day and serving the Lord together was just that—only a dream. And there were days when he was tempted to give up the dream. For one thing, there was Sumei to consider. She was a very attractive young woman who did strange things to his heart. They often talked about their painful experiences of the war and the tragedies that had engulfed them, but he had never mentioned his promise to Meiling to her.

"You seem very moody today," Sumei remarked one day. "Is something wrong?"

He looked into her questioning eyes and his heart skipped a beat. He had to admit that this lovely young woman with the long, swaying hair had gradually become extremely attractive to him. Struggling with his hopeless dilemma about Meiling, he suddenly realized how much Sumei's friendship meant to him. She was a godly young woman whose heart was drawn to wholeheartedly serving God.

She's so much like Meiling, he thought. *Just the kind of woman I would like to marry.* His thoughts were racing wildly in all directions as he contemplated an answer to her question. He sighed as he looked into her eyes.

"Yes," he answered hesitantly, fumbling for just the right words. "I'm struggling with a great problem. I guess I never told you about Meiling, the girl who led me to Christ up in Puyang many years ago."

Sumei looked at him with apprehension suddenly gripping her heart.

"Is she more than a high school friend of long ago?" she asked, as her throat tightened. She realized in that moment that she, too, had become very attracted to this fine young man.

"When I was conscripted into the army," he said slowly, "she ran alongside of the truck I was leaving in, and we clasped hands for as long as possible. I made a promise that day to find her again—even if it took the rest of my life."

There. It was finally off his chest. He had not meant to hide it from her, but there never had been an opportunity to talk about it until today. Sumei stood still, her heart pierced by his words. She fumbled for a response.

"So, Meiling is back in China somewhere, but you don't know where she is or if she is even alive. Is that right?" she probed, haltingly.

"That's right," he confessed, relieved that at last Sumei knew the whole story. "And I have determined to keep my promise, but it is so hard."

"But suppose she died in the war? Or suppose you can never return to China?" she questioned. "Will you still try to keep your promise, even though it might be impossible to ever meet her again?"

"Coming to know you," he said honestly, "has made my promise more and more difficult. I constantly ask myself those same questions and wonder whether it is foolish to cling to my promise."

"And when you pray about this matter, what does God say to you?" she asked, with anxiety in her voice.

"That's the problem, Sumei. God keeps impressing on my heart that Meiling is alive, and that I should keep my promise, difficult as it may be."

Sumei's eyes glistened with tears as she looked down at the ground, knowing that this man who sought God for everything in his life was a man of unusual integrity. He would keep his word and wait for Meiling; she knew it.

He watched her expression change, and he saw the tear that fell from her cheek.

"I'm so very sorry, Sumei," he said with a catch in his voice. "I never meant to hurt you, but for the present, I believe God is leading me to keep my promise."

"I understand," she replied. "You must do what you believe God wants you to do."

She slowly turned and walked away.

Chapter 5

THE RED GUARDS TAKE OVER

Tension in Taiping continued to mount after Sister Sung's death, as the Communists tightened control over every aspect of life in that city. The little church was confiscated and turned into a storage building. The cross that adorned the front of the building was painted over as authorities attempted to remove all vestiges of Christianity from the country.

Believers felt frightened and bewildered. First they lost their beloved Bible Woman and now their church building. Only after Elder Chu spent several days going from house to house, passing along the encouraging word that Meiling had consented to become the Bible Woman for the Taiping Church, did their spirits begin to lift.

"They have closed our church," Meiling said to the small group of people meeting in secret places during the night, "and they have destroyed our Bibles and hymnbooks, but they can never take the Word of God from our hearts! Dear friends," she admonished them, "keep memorizing Scripture every day... for the difficult times that are still ahead of us."

The days were darker than ever and no one was safe. Each community had a political cadre, whose responsibility it was to cleanse the thinking of the people and get family and neighbors to spy on each other. Rewards were offered for information about those who clung to the old ideas or in some way broke Mao's law. A new movement among young people known as the "Red Guards" was encouraged by Mao Zedong to cleanse the land of all old ideas and relics of the past.

Schools had been closed for several years and the wild gangs of restless teens that roamed the streets of many cities and towns wrecked havoc wherever they went. Cadres steeped in Communism whipped up the impressionable teens into a powerful force of destruction and chaos. They marched through the streets, forty or fifty young people to a gang, waving banners and shouting Mao's slogans. As the beat of their drums approached, people hurriedly shut their doors and gathered their children around them in fear that they would be their next target. Releasing the fanatic Red Guards was a clever plan to keep people in check.

Old Tang, as he was called, was a clever old man who had survived many conflicts in his war torn country. He was not above stealing a small bag of grain from the commune where he worked as a farm hand any time an opportunity came his way, but one day the ever-present, watchful eyes of a spy observed him sneaking along the path from the granary to his home.

The very next afternoon, a band of Red Guards marched to the beat of their drums down one of the streets in Taiping, as frantic people rushed to close up their homes. The incessant beat of the drums, accompanied by the shouts of the fanatical young people, came closer and closer to Old Tang's home, until they had surrounded it. Pounding on the door, they demanded entrance, and when the door was not opened they used their hammers and crowbars to force their way inside. All they knew was that he had been seen during the night with a small bag slung over his shoulder. They tore into the little house and, breaking up the little bit of furniture he had, they piled all of his belongings in the middle of the street and set them on fire.

"Where is the bag you brought here last night," they screamed, as they pulled the old man from his hiding place. Looking around for ways to torment the poor man, one of the Red Guards noticed a farmer with two large buckets of human waste he was carrying to the field for fertilizer. Shouting to his leader, he pointed to the man with the buckets. That was all that was needed. Tying the old man's hands behind his back, they forced him to sit in the middle of the road. Then they ordered the farmer to dump the contents of the buckets over Old Tang. They screamed and danced with delight at the sight of the old man being so humiliated.

When Meiling heard about the incident later that day she wondered if she would be next. She had been the Bible Woman in Taiping for four years now, making her a likely target. Every day the Red Guards moved up and down the streets of the town, seeking to wreck destruction on anyone who, in their opinion, was part of the Old China. She didn't have long to wait. While praying in her room one day for the needs of the flock God had entrusted to her, she heard the ominous sound of approaching drums. The commotion grew louder and louder until it reached her small home. She peeked out of the window, careful not to be seen. To her dismay, she saw them—thirty or more young people with red bands on their arms.

Instinctively, she cried out in prayer, *"Oh, God, they're coming to my home! Give me strength to stand this test and help me to glorify You."* The incessant pounding on her door shook the whole house, as the group shouted Mao slogans urging people to forsake all religion as it was "an opiate of the people." Opening the door, she was pushed rudely aside by the young people, who soon turned everything upside down.

"Where is that forbidden book?" they cried loudly. "We know you are a Christian and that you have a Bible. Give it to us or we will burn down your house!"

She was pulled in one direction and then another by the zealous teens, until her jacket was torn from her body. No one waited for an answer; they just pulled out everything she owned and piled it in the street. Long ago she had scooped out a hole in the dirt floor under her bed and built a secret receptacle for her precious Bible. Each night she carefully wrapped it in cloth and tucked it into the hiding place, with a prayer that God would preserve His Word.

Now Meiling stood in the street, as the young people set fire to her few possessions. The legs of the little table that she used for eating and studying were broken off. Fearfully, she watched as the flames consumed her belongings.

"Oh God," she prayed, *"don't let them find my Bible. It is one of the few we have left for our band of believers. What will we do if they find it?"*

She saw her bed being pushed out the door. It was a typical bed, made of slats of wood on which she spread out her bedding. She gasped as she watched them heave the slats onto the flames.

"I can sleep on the floor," she told God, *"but Lord, don't let them find the hiding place for my Bible. Preserve Your Word for Your people."*

She fervently prayed, but suddenly, above the din of voices, she heard excited shouting from inside her house. They had found her Bible!

Shouting with excitement at having found such damning evidence, the frenzied young people poured out of the house, holding up the large Bible for all to see. Then, with great gusto they tore out its pages and threw them into the flames. Finally they heaved what was left of her precious Bible into the roaring flames!

They watched for a few minutes with great satisfaction as the angry flames licked at the pages of the Bible, and then, when everything was consumed in the flames, they picked up their drums once again and started on down the street, with barely a look in her direction—intent on their next victim. As the beat of the drums faded in the distance, neighbors slowly ventured out to watch the dying flames. They turned silently and retreated to the safety of their homes, afraid to offer any assistance lest they be reported and become the next victim of the Red Guards.

Meiling stood alone in the doorway of her empty home.

"Oh, Lord," she prayed, *"turn this great loss into blessing somehow. I trust you, even though I do not understand why this has happened. Like so many things in these past years, I have no explanation for them, but I know that You are still in charge and that You will be exalted—even in this disaster!"*

Meiling made her way to Elder Chu's home and related every detail of the sad story.

"My child," he said, "even though Satan has won this battle, he can never win the war! Jesus is Victor. We will go on, and the church will prosper. One day the world will be amazed at the strength of the Chinese Church that could not be broken by this awful persecution."

Early the next morning Elder Chu accompanied Meiling back to her humble home. There in the street was the blackened pile of ashes—all that remained of her possessions and her Bible. Elder Chu looked at her ruined home with sadness in his eyes.

"My dear Meiling, I encouraged you to become our Bible Woman a few years ago. All I could promise you was that God would be your Helper and your strength for these awful days. May He encourage you right now and give you the assurance that He is still on the throne and in control of all things."

"I do not mind the loss of my possessions," she responded, "but only my Bible," she said mournfully. "We must begin to copy down the Scriptures by hand," she added as a new thought struck her. "We must never lose the power of God's Word."

"You are right, Meiling," said Elder Chu. "We must begin right away. Thank God we still have my Bible. I must redouble my efforts to memorize it so that I will have it no matter what happens."

As Elder Chu stood looking sadly at the ash heap, Meiling picked up a stick and began to stir the blackened ashes. As she stirred them, the stick touched a hard object. Pushing the object out of the ashes, she bent over and picked up the blackened mass. Her heart leapt with excitement.

"Look, Elder Chu," she called excitedly, "here's a book, and it looks like my Bible!" Not much remained of the precious book but, blowing aside the ashes, she gasped when she saw some legible words leaping at her out of the ashes.

"Elder Chu, come quickly. Look. Look what it says! 'The gates of hell shall not prevail!'" (Matthew 16:18)

Elder Chu carefully took the fragments from her hands and looked intently at the barely legible words.

"Meiling, do you realize what this says?" he asked excitedly. "Satan has done his worst, but just as I said a few minutes ago, Jesus is Victor. Here it is on this charred page: 'The gates of hell shall not prevail!' Oh, praise God, neither Satan nor the Communists can blot out the Church of Jesus Christ. What a promise and what a testimony to encourage our hearts in the midst of this storm!" Together, they gave thanks.

The believers rallied around their beloved Meiling and brought various items from their meager possessions to help her get established once again. Yo, a young mother about Meiling's age, was a fervent believer. At the secret meetings of the believers, she carefully copied down the Scriptures that were read as she prepared her own handwritten portion of God's Word.

"I have come to help restore your home," she said, slipping inside the little home, now empty of furniture but cluttered with papers and pictures scattered all over the floor.

"Oh, what a terrible mess, Sister Meiling," she said as she looked around the room. "All of your possessions are gone—destroyed by those wicked young people!"

"But you have heard about my Bible and the verse God preserved, haven't you?" responded Meiling. "It's so amazing that God preserved the words: 'The gates of hell shall not prevail.' They were preserved by God to encourage us to know that even when Satan does his worst he will not overcome us. We must believe this promise!"

"Yes, I do believe it," Yo responded, "but this is awful. You have nothing left."

"Oh, I have more than you can imagine. I have Jesus in my heart, and He satisfies me, even though I have lost everything." Meiling's face shone with certainty as she spoke.

"You have helped me so much," replied Yo, as she knelt on the floor to gather up papers and personal items scattered all over. "You are God's messenger to me. You have helped me so much to overcome the disappointments of my life. I thank God for you every day and pray that I will be as faithful a follower of Jesus as you are."

"You never need to be like me, Yo, only be like Jesus," Meiling responded sincerely. "Just obey Him at all times, and you will grow to be like Him."

Yo picked up a picture from the pile of things scattered all over the floor. Looking at it for several moments, she gasped and cried out in shocked amazement.

"Meiling, I know this man. He saved my life!"

Meiling looked up to see Sister Yo sitting on the floor, holding a faded picture of Anching that she had preserved over the years.

"You know Anching?" she exclaimed excitedly. "How could you?

Yo sat staring at Anching's picture.

"Meiling, I could never forget him. This is the man who saved my baby's life after that last battle when my husband was killed. He was pulling his wounded friend on a cart from the battlefield up north, hoping to reach the mission hospital here in Taiping. When we parted, he gave me his New Testament; the one I have read every day."

"This is unbelievable," Meiling responded excitedly, as she sat down on the floor amidst the papers. "I had no idea you knew Anching!"

"Is he your brother or a relative?" asked Yo, with a quizzical look on her face. Meiling blushed conspicuously. "Judging by your face, I would say he is more than a brother, right?" Yo laughingly said as she observed Meiling's reaction.

"Oh, Yo," she smiled wistfully, "he is the man I have loved for many years. The last time I saw him was over fifteen years ago, when I ran alongside the truck that whisked him so suddenly out of my life. To this day his last words to me ring in my ears every day—even after all these years! 'Meiling,' he called. 'I will find you if it takes the rest of my life!'"

Meiling buried her face in her hands and wept softly. Yo put her arm around her heaving shoulders and held her tightly. Time escaped them as they sat together on the floor, while Yo related all the details of her encounter with Anching. They both laughed as she recounted the episode when she pretended to be his wife and they escaped through enemy lines with his wounded friend under the hay.

"I never knew their names," she mused, "but I could never forget their faces or their words about Jesus. They urged me to seek out the believers in the town near where my parents lived and to follow Jesus. I did, and I have never regretted it. I will be in heaven someday because of those two men."

Meiling wiped the tears from her eyes and smiled at her friend.

"That is the best news I have heard in years," she said. "A missionary friend of my pastor in Puyang passed through our town several months after Anching was taken. He told us that Anching and two friends had helped to protect thirty blind women in the Home for the Blind the night the troops took over the place. I was so proud of him, and now you have added another thrilling chapter from his life. I have no idea where he is, although I presume he tried to escape to Hong Kong. We were so certain that God wanted us to serve Him together that I have held on to his last words, 'I will find you even if it takes the rest of my life.'"

She bowed her head and wept more tears. After a few minutes, she regained her composure and spoke. "I believe that God has preserved him as He has me, and that we will meet again someday and serve the Lord together. I will also wait for him for the rest of my life."

The story of Yo's discovery of Anching's picture at Meiling's ruined home spread rapidly among the believers. Elder Chu nodded knowingly to his wife.

"Now I understand why she is so adamant about remaining single. Remember how she turned down the offer of marriage I tried to arrange for her with Pastor Qi?" he said, with a twinkle in his eyes.

"She is a beautiful woman inside and out. I know there have been several fine Christian men who wished to marry her. I could never quite figure out why she always said she was not interested. Her usual response was that she was too busy serving God's people to think of marriage. Now I understand. This Anching must be a marvelous man to inspire such a commitment."

The Red Guards rampaged through Taiping week after week with no one to restrain them. Those who opposed them were ridiculed and subjected to barbarous acts of violence and vandalism. The whole land of China was in the grip of these lawless young people who were encouraged by Mao Zedong to wipe out the past and prepare for the New China. This was one of the worst disasters that occurred in China as many priceless artifacts were destroyed by the indiscriminate rampaging. Mao calculated that the Red Guards would purge the land and accomplish his purpose, but he never anticipated the extremes that swept the land as one group tried to outdo the other. Even Communist officials dared not resist them, lest they in turn be subjected to the humiliation they wrecked on anyone who stood in their way. It was one of the darkest periods of the Revolution and a time when the believers were forced deeper and deeper underground.

Except for one or two showplaces in Beijing and Shanghai every church was shut down, turned into a storage place, or willfully vandalized. Despite the fact that it was more and more dangerous to meet together, the believers sought every opportunity to do so—regardless of personal cost.

Like Sister Sung before her, Meiling trudged from place to place and town to town to nurture the flock, even though it was becoming increasingly more dangerous to do so. Elder Chu and his wife were much concerned for her safety, but she insisted that the Lord would take care of her and sustain her in the worsening circumstances of the country. On this night, she was once more cautiously making her way to the designated meeting place—the words of Psalm 46 running through her mind. There was only one precious Bible left among the more than one hundred believers of the area, but no one was deterred from devouring the Word. Each brought paper and pen to record the passage being used. Slowly and meticulously, each wrote the characters down, to be added to their own personal, handwritten Bibles, which they were developing to replace the ones destroyed by the Red Guards.

Every precaution was taken to preserve the one Bible among them by making certain that it never remained in the same home for more than a week. Each trusted family had developed a secret hiding place for this Bible, and once the passage was read and written down, the book was quickly returned to its hiding place. As an additional precaution, only one person in each family knew just where the Bible was hidden.

Meiling eagerly greeted the believers as she quietly entered the house. As soon as the small group had gathered, she began teaching, using their one Bible. As she finished reading the first verse, "The Lord Almighty is with us; the God of Jacob is our refuge," suddenly the quietness of the night was broken by loud shouting and pounding on the door. Everyone in the room knew what that dreaded sound meant. Almost in unison they whispered the words again, "The Lord Almighty is with us!"

Meiling realized the seriousness of the situation and quickly passed the Bible to the evening's host, who disappeared immediately to deposit the Bible in its secret hiding place. They would be beaten, no doubt, but the precious Bible must be safeguarded for another time, when it would bring encouragement and hope.

A contingent of policemen burst into the room and, with flashlights blinding the eyes of the frightened believers, they handcuffed and shoved them roughly out to the waiting police van. Arriving at the police station, Meiling was quickly identified as the leader and separated from the rest. As she was being led away, she looked toward the others and said confidently, "Remember, God is our refuge and strength—an ever-present help in trouble" (Psalm 46:1).

"Move on," shouted an officer rudely as he gave Meiling a rough shove toward the door. It slammed behind her and she found herself being pushed down the hallway. Suddenly her whole body was wracked with searing pain as the officer prodded her with an electric stick. She stumbled, as the current surged through her body.

"Move! Move!" shouted the officer, who prodded her again, sending another powerful shock through her body.

"Oh God," she breathed in prayer, *"help me to stand true to You under this attack. Make me a bold witness, and help me not to bring shame on Your Name."*

At the end of the hallway, a door opened to a row of cells. She was rudely prodded and shoved into one dank cell. She fell to the floor in a daze and lay there for several minutes. Slowly, she pushed herself up to a kneeling position and surveyed the room. It was tiny—only six by eight feet—with only a single cot and the familiar toilet bucket. She crawled to the cot and pulled herself up weakly, still feeling the aftereffects of the electric shock treatment.

Flopping down on the hard, bare cot, she breathed a sigh of relief that she had made it to the bed. Then in the stillness of the room she heard the familiar voice of her Lord whispering in her heart. *"My grace is sufficient for you, for my power is made perfect in weakness."* (2 Corinthians 12:9)

"Yes, dear Lord," she whispered aloud, "I lean on Your strength to transform my weakness into a powerful testimony for You. Help me to stand the test and bring glory to Your Name."

Meiling lay there a long time, until sleep finally took over and brought much-needed rest to her exhausted body. It was still dark when a bright ceiling light was turned on that began to blink on and off rapidly.

What new torture can they think of now? she thought, as she shielded her eyes from the blinding light. It continued for an interminable time; perhaps thirty minutes, until it seemed like spots of different color blinded her. As quickly as the light started blinking, it stopped, and darkness once again enveloped her—only now her vision had been distorted by the blinding light, so that she could no longer distinguish anything.

The cell door creaked opened and she was ordered to stand up and follow. Her problem was that she could hear the voice, but see nothing. A hand reached out and pulled her forward. She stepped out blindly, not daring to hesitate lest she be prodded again by the electric stick. After a few moments she was shoved down into a chair and left alone to stare, while the bright spots continued to flash before her eyes. How long she sat there, she did not know, but gradually the spots began to disappear, allowing her to see the dim outline of a well-furnished room.

This must be the office of a special official, she thought, as she tried to gain a perspective on her surroundings. The clock on the wall read 7:35. *I've been in police custody since 3 A.M.* she thought. *Interrogation will be starting soon. Oh, Jesus, help me to be strong and faithful to You, no matter what happens,"* she prayed silently.

The door opened and an impeccably dressed officer walked in and sat down behind the desk. Meiling squinted to make out his features. *Why was she to be interrogated by such a high-ranking police official?* she wondered. She could not make out his features very clearly, but there was something familiar about this man. *Where had she met him before?*

"So, we meet again, Woo Meiling," began the voice. Her heart froze. She could never forget that voice. Fear flooded her heart in that moment.

"*Oh, God,"* she prayed, "*if ever I needed You before, I need You now!"* Her heart was pounding and her mind reeled with surprise and fear.

At that moment the unseen Presence of the Lord enveloped her, and her troubled heart quieted as she leaned on Him. *My child*, the voice in her heart resounded, *I am with you. Do not be afraid. I will never leave you.* Strengthened, she sat upright, facing her accuser with a confidence she didn't know she possessed.

"I guess you never expected to meet me again," the voice said with a smirk. "I also never expected to meet you again, and especially as the leader of a forbidden Christian group. But then, on the other hand, I'm not surprised. You were always on the wrong side from the beginning, weren't you? Do you recognize me in this fine uniform and in this richly furnished office?"

Meiling said nothing, as the realization of who the man was registered sharply. His features became visible with her clearing vision. *Yes, she knew him all right.* Fear gripped her heart momentarily as she realized her predicament. *How could she ever forget him? He had aged, of course, but he was still the same arrogant man who had caused her so much trouble.*

"Come, come, surely you haven't forgotten me," he smirked. "You had the audacity to step between Anching and me years ago and protect that poor peasant; don't you remember?" he glared. "The Pang Luping you despised in those days now sits as your judge. Imagine the turn of events? You see, I made the right choice after all. I'm in charge here now, and you're a prisoner," Pang continued, smacking his lips with self-satisfaction.

Meiling said nothing. He had not asked her any direct question that needed an answer, but all the fury that once filled her heart for this despicable man again flooded her mind. The painful memory of Anching overwhelmed her as she sat tense and waiting.

"So, you do remember me, don't you?" he asked directly and waited for an answer.

"Yes, I do," she replied softly. Then, gaining confidence from the Lord, she continued. "But, Luping..." she started, and then hesitated. "Oh, please forgive me. I don't know your title."

"I'm the Chief of Police for this county," he filled in, with an air of pride that brought a rush of memories back to her. *He hasn't changed one bit*, she thought, as his arrogance came through loud and clear.

"You should address me as Chief Pang from now on," he added with a laugh. "And remember, you can't run to your father for help now," he said with a half growl in his voice. "Obviously, you and that peasant made the wrong choice. I suppose he's dead by now," he added cruelly. The thought sent a stab of pain through her being as she shuddered at his callousness.

"Where is he?" he demanded.

Meiling pursed her lips to answer, as a wave of uncertainty swept through her being. She had never been afraid of this wimp of a man in former days, but today was different. He sat in the place of authority, and she wondered what he would do.

Hesitating for a moment, she answered.

"I do not know. I have never heard from him since that day he was taken into the army." She hesitated. *Should she say what was in her mind; that she remembered how Luping had gotten off because of his rich father?*

Pang sensed her hesitation. He prodded her.

"Go ahead and say it. I know what you're thinking. You're thinking, 'Your father bought you freedom while Anching went to war.' In that moment of hesitation he shouted loudly, "That's what you're thinking, aren't you?" he demanded.

Lifting her heart in silent prayer Meiling answered. "Yes, Chief Pang, I know you made the wrong choice! You sit here today in a place of authority, but you don't have any peace in your heart. It is still as empty as ever—even though your pockets are full of money and the government has vested you with authority."

His face flushed with boiling anger. He jumped from his seat and walked menacingly towards her.

"You will never change, will you? You're still full of those crazy ideas that sent your father to prison and you into exile? Believe me, I made the right decision," he shouted angrily, "and I'm in control today. That proves it!"

He hovered threateningly over her, but even though she could feel his hot breath on her face, there was a strange sense of peace in her heart. As she had experienced in other interrogations, she sensed that she was actually the one in charge and the man in front of her was frightened and threatened by a woman prisoner. Gaining control of his emotions, he spoke more civilly, changing the subject.

"That's enough of those ridiculous theories," he said firmly. "Let's get on with this interrogation." Reaching into the drawer of his desk, he shoved some sheets of paper towards her." Take a look at these sheets," he said, as confidence returned to him. "These sheets were found in the possession of some of your Christians. I want you to identify them and confirm what I already know. These are portions from the Bible. Isn't that correct?" he sneered. "And don't try to deny where they came from. We found these in a Christian's home, and she confessed that she wrote down what you had dictated."

Meiling glanced at the sheets before her, as her heart pounded with excitement. Chief Pang intended to frighten her with this evidence, but instead her heart leaped for joy. There before her were verses from the Bible, Jeremiah 29:10, 11, a passage she had explained to the people several weeks ago.

"Oh, thank You, Jesus," she breathed silently. *"This is your message of hope to me right now!"*

"Well, do you admit that this is from that forbidden book, the Bible?" he fumed irritably, as he waited for her answer. "Is this from the Bible? And did you read this to people and have them write it down?" he pressed.

She took her time in answering, savoring the miracle that brought these wonderful words to her at just the right moment. Then, lifting her head she questioned him. "Do you mean these words? 'I will come to you and fulfill My gracious promise to bring you back to this place, for I know the plans I have for you,' declares the Lord, 'plans to prosper you and not to harm you, plans to give you hope and a future.'"

Her eyes danced with delight. Right here in the lion's den, God had spoken His promise to her, and given her the opportunity to read it to a powerful Communist official.

Chief Pang instantly recognized how skillfully she had picked out a phrase that had struck him right in the face, as if she had hit him with a hammer.

"You insolent, scheming counterrevolutionary," he screamed, using the name the government tagged on anyone who opposed them. "I didn't ask you to read it to me. I asked if it was from the Bible…and did you read it to a group of people?" He approached her boldly and slapped her across the mouth. Smiling with satisfaction, he blurted out, "There! That's what I've wanted to do for years! Ever since you humiliated me before my friends years ago."

Meiling's mouth throbbed, but a song welled up in her heart. Jesus had brought her a special message, right here in a Communist's office, and she had read it boldly to him. She knew he had been pricked by the scripture's message.

"You haven't answered my question," he continued shouting. "Don't think you can hide it from me," he said, as he again smacked her hard on the face. "Answer me, or you will be made to answer."

Meiling answered quietly, but with growing confidence.

"Yes, I have read those verses many times and I have encouraged people to write them down, and even to memorize them. They bring great comfort to my heart, and they can bring you the peace you need, as well."

The chief clenched his fist and hit her in the eye, knocking her to the floor.

"Get up, you stinking pig," he shouted, as he kicked her in the ribs. Gasping for breath, Meiling pulled herself up on the chair and waited for another blow. Just then the telephone rang, interrupting another blow. The chief listened for a moment, and then asked questions rapidly.

"He was hit by a car?" he asked, with trembling voice. "Is he alive?" He listened anxiously and then, pressing a button on his desk, he summoned a junior police officer. "Take the prisoner back to her cell. I must leave immediately," he ordered. Then, with a quiver in his voice, he continued.

"My son was struck by a car and may not live."

Meiling breathed with relief. The interrogation was over. God had intervened again. As she left the room with the guard, her heart was flooded with praise. God had spoken to her from some random pages of Scripture on the chief's ' desk, and she had been comforted.

A couple of weeks passed slowly as Meiling waited for the next encounter. There was only a faint shadow remaining of the black eye she had suffered at the hands of Luping, but she rejoiced as she realized again that God had not forsaken her in her hour of need. Now, standing before Luping once again, she marveled at the strength that flowed through her body. *What surprise does God have in store for me today,* she wondered, as she waited for Luping to speak.

Without looking at her, he said in a subdued voice: "You can go free as soon as you tell me where the Bible is being hidden and who owns it."

"I cannot tell you where the Bible is because I do not know," she answered courageously. "It is a secret known only to the person who has the Bible, and as to who owns it, I can tell you only this: It belongs to all of the believers, not just to one person."

"How can you be so insolent when answering me?" he asked with astonishment. "Don't you know yet that I have authority over your life; that you are in my control and that there is no one to come to your rescue?"

"I only know this fact, Chief Pang," she answered, candidly. "Jesus is my refuge at all times. He has never forsaken me for even one moment. He is here right now to strengthen and protect me."

"Ha!" he exclaimed haughtily, as he picked up a heavy piece of rope on his desk. Swinging it viciously, he scoffed.

"Where is your God now?" The heavy rope struck her shoulder with a hissing sound, causing her to stagger. Another blow landed on her hips, sending searing pain through her whole body.

"So your God is here, is He?" shouted Luping. "Well, where is He? Let him set you free right now," he shouted, raining several blows upon her helpless body.

The telephone rang, interrupting his tirade.

"What?" he asked in disbelief. "Let me talk with her."

"Luping," the voice spoke into the telephone, "are you beating someone again in your office? I feel the pain in my own body. When will you stop this frenzied beating of the Christians? They have never hurt you. It is the Communists whom you now serve that hung your father by his thumbs. Do you remember that? Now stop this beating and come and help me. Your old mother needs you now, or I fear I will die."

Stunned, he placed the receiver in its cradle and, with a puzzled look on his face, said, "That was my mother. You remember her, don't you? She is very ill and needs my help. I must go now and help her."

Laying the rope down on his desk, Luping walked silently out of the room. In a few minutes, the door opened and an officer entered, carrying a parcel and some papers in his hand.

"Here are all of the belongings you had when you were arrested," he said matter-of-factly. Sign this paper, stating that they were all returned to you, and then you are free to go."

Meiling was stunned by the sudden turn of events. It took her a few moments to realize that God had once again intervened to free her. Signing the paper and picking up her belongings, she turned and walked out of the police station a free woman.

Her mysterious release three weeks earlier continued to puzzled Meiling. *What had caused the sudden change in Luping?* she wondered day after day, *and what would be happening next?* Her thoughts were interrupted by someone knocking on her door. Opening it briskly, she was shocked to see a young police officer standing there with an envelope in his hand. Bowing politely, he offered her the envelope, excused himself, and left. Meiling closed the door and sat down, turning the envelope over and over in her hands.

Now what is this all about? she thought, pensively. *The police officer was so polite and made no demands, which in itself was most unusual!* Puzzled, she bowed her head and prayed.

"Lord Jesus, whatever this is about, please help me and give me the wisdom to deal with it. She slowly opened the letter and read with growing surprise. It was from Luping!

"I don't know if you have it in your heart to do me a favor," the letter began, "but I would appreciate it very much if you would visit my mother. She is very ill and may not live much longer. In spite of what I have done to you, I know that you are the only one who has the real answer to life and death. Please come help my mother." It was signed simply, "Luping."

The next day Meiling took a bus to Luping's home, located in one of the best sections of the city, with some feelings of trepidation. *What is behind this sudden change of heart?* she wondered, as she approached the attractive home that only prominent officials could afford. Luping himself opened the door and let her in, speaking as he closed the door.

"You Christians have always amazed me. Why would you be so kind as to come to visit my mother when I have treated you so badly? That's the same quality I saw in Anching years ago and it infuriated me. After all these years, I am still puzzled," he added, honestly.

Sensing an unusual openness and honesty in his comment, Meiling replied without hesitation, "I admit that it is not natural to be kind to someone who has wronged you, but it is possible because Jesus lives within me. He gives me the grace to love my enemies and to pray for them."

"I know that," asserted Luping. "Anching said that to me many times when I tried to provoke a fight with him. I hated him for it, but deep down inside I knew that he was right, and that he was the better man because of it. Now you have demonstrated it again, and I am deeply moved."

The expression on his face revealed something Meiling had never seen before—honesty and heartfelt emotion. Embarrassed that he had revealed this deep emotion, he quickly recovered control of himself.

"Come, my mother is waiting to see you again."

Meiling entered the room and saw a shadow of the Mrs. Pang she had known years earlier. She knelt by her bedside and embraced her as memories of her own mother overwhelmed her with emotion.

"Oh, Mrs. Pang," she exclaimed, choking back the tears, "it has been so long since I have seen you! So much has happened since we all lived in Puyang."

"Oh, my dear Meiling, you are as beautiful as ever, and you, too, have suffered. I am afraid that much of your suffering has been at the hands of my son, Luping. I am ashamed of him," she said, as she looked directly at him standing by her bedside. "He has been consumed with a passion to exterminate the Christians of China. I have warned him that he is causing my death by his wicked deeds."

Luping said nothing but stood by the bedside with bowed head and downcast eyes.

"Mrs. Pang," Meiling hastened to explain, "except for the mercy of God at work in me, I could be as capable of those same deeds as anyone else. The only thing that makes a difference is Jesus living in me."

She looked up at Luping. *Is that a tear in his eye? His face is contorted with pain.*

"Oh, God," she prayed silently, *"let this be the time he opens his heart to You!"*

Mrs. Pang saw her son's reaction, too. She gripped Meiling's hand and pleaded with her. "Tell us, Meiling, how can we find this same peace you have experienced that has changed your life so much? I am dying with cancer, and I do not have much time left in this world. Tell me how to find the way to God."

The beatings she had received at the hands of Luping and the black eye that had discolored her face for days seemed like nothing as her heart leaped with joy because of Mrs. Pang's question. Meiling spent the next hour explaining the way to God through Jesus Christ, using simple language that Mrs. Pang could understand.

When she was finished, Mrs. Pang prayed a prayer of repentance. Luping sat by her bedside the entire time, listening.

Should she speak to him about receiving Christ? she wondered. Her thoughts were interrupted by Luping.

"Thank you for coming to visit my mother. You have helped her so much. Now, please pray that your God will heal her and allow me time to make up to her for the years I have neglected her and spurned her advice and love."

"I will," Meiling replied, with deep feeling, "and I will also pray that you too will accept Jesus, as your mother has."

"Meiling, you don't have any idea how dangerous that would be for me. At least for now, I am thankful that my mother has found the peace you have. Maybe someday I can follow, also." He paused and, looking at Meiling, he spoke quietly. "That was a most dangerous thing for me to say. Please do not repeat it or I will be a dead man."

"Luping," she responded, "it is better to die for Jesus than to live in a false security that is so temporary. The sufferings I have endured are nothing compared to the joy that is waiting for me in heaven. Oh, I hope the day will soon come when you, too, will follow Jesus."

Leading her to the door, he said simply, "Please be careful. What you are doing is very dangerous. This government will stop at nothing in order to eliminate all Christians." He closed the door behind her.

As she turned to make her way home, she fairly leaped for joy that Mrs. Pang had found the Savior. She marveled at the change she had observed in Luping, and she prayed for his salvation with renewed faith. God was indeed a God of miracles!

Chapter 6

REUNION

Life was never easy in the dampness and cold of the coal mines of Datung, where prisoners spent twelve hours a day at hard labor. Meiling's father, Principal Woo, had spent nearly ten years at hard labor in what the Communists called a "reeducation program for counter-revolutionaries." During that time he endured grueling work in the mines, as well as inhumane and brutal treatment day after day.

The presence of Pastor Wong, an elderly evangelist, had made life bearable by his constant words of encouragement. Through almost seventeen years of incarceration this man with the indomitable spirit of joy and hope had led hundreds of men to new life and hope in Jesus. But the harsh winters and the cruel treatment had taken their toll on his frail body. It was during the winter of Mr. Woo's seventh year of confinement that Pastor Wong had become very ill with pneumonia and died. A pall of sorrow swept through the ranks of the prisoners as they realized their only link with hope no longer existed.

For Mr. Woo, who had leaned so heavily on the prayers and teaching of the frail pastor, it seemed as though the last glimmer of light in this dungeon had been snuffed out. Destitute, lonely, and suffering with painful rheumatism himself, he wept uncontrollably, like so many others, when news of the pastor's death spread. He was consoled only by the words of the Apostle Paul, which Pastor Wong had quoted more and more frequently during his last days, reminding them that "to be absent from the body is to be present with the Lord" (2 Corinthians 5:6).

"Brother Woo," he would say, "the days of my pilgrimage are drawing to a close. I will soon rest in the arms of my Lord and Savior. Do not mourn for me, because at last I will be home, where this endless pain and sorrow can no longer touch me. Rejoice that I am with Jesus, but be faithful unto death yourself. Someday we will meet in the presence of our wonderful Lord."

"But how can I go on?" Mr. Woo asked sorrowfully. "You have been my strength and my hope in this miserable darkness."

"Ah, no, my dear brother," he said, reaching out his bony fingers to grip his arm, "Jesus is your strength and your hope, a very present help in time of trouble (Psalm 46:1). I have only been His instrument. Now I am passing my mantle on to you. Watch over the brothers here in this place—and turn their eyes back to Jesus at all times."

The words rang in Mr. Woo's heart like a clarion bell peeling forth its message of hope. He watched the dejected men, like zombies, pick up their axes and go listlessly about their endless task of meeting the day's quota. With no hope left in them, they worked more and more slowly, only to receive the lashes of the foreman for failing to meet the quota.

"What's wrong with you lazy dogs?" the foreman screamed, as he beat them unmercifully.

Mr. Woo felt the sting of the whip because his team was failing to measure up. Nursing his wounds, he cried out to God. *Oh, God, if only Pastor Wong were here! He would have a word of encouragement for us all!*

Quietly in his heart he heard the voice of Jesus respond. *"Remember Pastor Wong's last words to you? 'The Lord is your strength and your hope. I have only been His instrument. Now I am passing the mantle on to you.'"* Suddenly in the darkness of the mine it seemed like a light began to shine before his eyes, until the whole place was lit by the glorious Light and warmth of the Presence of Jesus. He sensed he was in the Holy Presence of the Living God and, like Moses standing by the burning bush, he bowed in surrender. By God's grace he would accept the challenge of being God's instrument of hope for the men in this prison. It was a defining moment in his life when he determined that, with God's help, he would be an instrument of hope and light in the darkness of the coal mine. The warmth of God's Presence lifted his spirit and comforted his weary body. As the vision slowly faded, Mr. Woo felt an urgency to share his renewed hope without delay.

"Men," he said to his teammates, "I have been overcome with my own sorrow and have failed to follow the instructions of Pastor Wong to me before He entered the Presence of Jesus. Forgive me for failing you and my Lord, but from now on I am here to speak the words of hope and comfort to you from God's Word. My God just reminded me of the great promise the prophet Isaiah gave to the people of Israel when they felt destitute and forsaken. The Lord spoke to them and said, 'Fear not, for I have redeemed you; I have summoned you by name; you are mine. When you pass through the waters, I will be with you; and when you pass through the rivers, they will not sweep over you. When you walk through the fire, you will not be burned; the flames will not set you ablaze. For I am the Lord, your God, the Holy One of Israel, your Savior'" (Isaiah 43:1, 2).

The men paused a moment and leaned upon their axes, mesmerized by the Word of hope given in the darkness. There were exclamations of joy.

"That's the first word of hope I have heard since Pastor Wong died," one man exclaimed.

"I feel better already," said another.

"I feel new strength in my heart," echoed a third, "and men, we can meet our quota today by the help of the Lord, who has spoken to us from His Word."

The men resumed their work with an energy that had been missing for several days. When the day was ended, the foreman remarked with surprise that they were one of the few teams that had met their quota. Walking back to their sleeping quarters, the team spread the word that Pastor Wong was back among them in the person of Mr. Woo!

The long days turned to weeks and months as Mr. Woo bravely shared the joy of the Lord with the men who labored in the bowels of the earth. For those who received the Word, there was hope in the midst of despair. For those who rejected it, there was only increasing despair, and for many only suicide.

Now as his term of ten years was drawing to a close, Mr. Woo searched for someone to whom he could pass Pastor Wong's mantle.

"The word of hope in this dark place must not waiver," he repeated again and again to a fellow prisoner whose heart the Lord had touched.

"I will soon pass the mantle on to you. Be faithful and encourage the men to rely upon God's Word alone. Then you will be lifted up in your own heart, and you will bring many to faith."

One day he was called into the superintendent's office and offered a chair.

"Woo," the superintendent began, "your term will be completed in one more month. I have been authorized to inform you that you will be free to return to your home. During these ten years that you have been here, you have been a model prisoner, and not once have you caused us any trouble. I commend you on your good behavior and hope that you have learned your lesson and will be a model Communist and supporter of our great leader Mao Zedong." He waited expectantly for a response.

Many things flashed through Mr. Woo's mind in those few seconds. *Give the party line. Don't say anything about your faith at this moment, or you will risk more years here. Tell him how much you love Mao.*

He licked his lips nervously as he remembered that the Bible declared that in these moments God would give the words to say.

"Comrade Superintendent," he began, "I have always loved my country and been a loyal citizen. I am grateful that I will be released, and I assure you that there will not be a more loyal citizen than me. I will support my country with all my heart, but you must know that no matter what happens, I will also follow Jesus, my Lord and my Savior."

He finished and waited for the axe to fall. After a few seconds of silence, the superintendent responded.

"Woo, that is what I expected you to say. I would have been shocked if you had answered any other way. I know that men like you and that old pastor who died a few years ago have changed this place and made life easier for me. Just be careful in the world outside. It is not the popular thing to believe as you do." He paused, and with a pleasant nod of his head he said, "That will be all for today."

Exhilarated, Mr. Woo returned to his dorm, confident that he would soon be released and on his way home to his wife and family.

The train puffed into the railroad station in Wuhan. Mr. Woo waited impatiently to get off and see his family again. *What would*

they look like after ten years? he wondered. *Would they recognize him?* His hair had turned white and his face was gaunt from years of deprivation and lack of sunlight; his back bent from years of working in the mine. *If they recognize me,* he thought, *it will be a miracle!*

As the train slowed to a halt he found himself stretching his neck in an attempt to catch a glimpse of his wife. Moving as quickly as possible, he stepped down off the train and anxiously scanned the sea of faces. *Could that be my wife,* he gasped, as a small woman bent with age waved her hand. *That can't be my wife. She's waving at someone else.* Then their eyes locked and they rushed as quickly as possible toward each other.

"Oh, my poor husband!" she exclaimed in dismay. "What have they done to you? You're so thin and your complexion is so unhealthy looking."

"Just what I was thinking about you!" he exclaimed. "I almost passed you by! But let's hurry home. We have so much to talk about."

"I'm sorry, but we don't have much of a home anymore," she replied sorrowfully, "but it is home, and it will be better now that you will be there."

Since her release from the commune Meiling received letters from her mother frequently, with news of the family always included. Meiling wept as she read her mother's letters that described her father's physical condition.

"Come as soon as you can," she wrote. "We can hardly wait to see you again."

"Lord," she prayed, "please open the door for me to go home for a visit."

Believing that the Lord was leading her, she applied for a travel permit. After three disappointing refusals, she was impressed while at prayer one day to speak with Mrs. Pang on her next visit.

"I will pray that Luping will help you," said Mrs. Pang, as she listened sympathetically to Meiling's desire to see her family.

"Ever since he called you to come and pray for me, I have noticed a great change in him. I know he has been very cruel to you and to all the Christians that have been arrested, but God did work a miracle in his heart when I was so sick. Now I am going to ask God to perform another miracle and cause him to grant you the travel permit."

"That would indeed be a miracle that only God could orchestrate," Meiling replied wistfully, "but I do believe that God can do anything."

Several uneventful weeks passed with still no response regarding a travel permit.

"I spoke with Luping a few days ago," Mrs. Pang reported when Meiling visited her again. "He simply said that it was not as easy as I might think. Meiling, I believe God is working in his heart. Now that I have accepted Jesus, I talk to him frequently about his need of God. He never refutes anything I say. He just listens quietly. Believe me, that is a miracle in itself! He has always been such a headstrong man, but I thank God that He is softening his heart."

A few days later a messenger boy delivered Meiling a travel permit, signed by Chief Pang, granting her a one-month visit to Puyang!

Will this train never reach Wuhan? Meiling anxiously thought as the countryside grew more and more familiar. *So many years filled with hurt and pain had passed. What will it be like to see my parents*

again? And the rest of the family? My parents have suffered so much and life is still so cruel to them, even though father has been released from prison. Oh, train, hurry up. I can hardly wait!

As the train slowed to a halt, she saw them: two elderly people, bent with age and gaunt from deprivation, standing side-by-side, straining their necks to catch a first glimpse of their beloved daughter. *Oh, God, how they have changed!*

Her thoughts were interrupted as they caught sight of her as she stepped off the train. Waving vigorously, they called out joyfully.

"Meiling! Meiling! Over here! Over here!" The old joy and zest for living seemed to surge back into them as they pushed their way toward her and gripped her in a long, passionate embrace. The crowd was forgotten as they hugged and talked excitedly.

"You are as beautiful as ever," her father kept exclaiming joyfully.

"Oh, my precious child," Mrs. Woo exclaimed, as she continued to tearfully hug her. "You are still so full of Jesus. I can see Him in you."

"Oh, mother…father! How good to see you again. Thank God, you are still alive! I almost despaired of ever seeing you again!"

As they made their way to their apartment Meiling wondered what it would be like. The area where they headed was run down and the streets crowded. Approaching some five-story buildings, Mr. Woo spoke to his daughter.

"Your mother was very fortunate to find a small apartment soon after I was sent to Datung. It is not like our former home, but she has made it into a place that is filled with the warmth of love. After the barracks at Datung, almost anything is better, and this is beautiful because we will all be together tonight for the first time in oh-so-many years."

Entering the narrow entrance, they climbed to the third floor. The furniture was the same that she remembered from years ago, but the apartment was small and gloomy, and the neighbors were close. It was nothing like the spacious home they had once enjoyed.

"Be careful what you say," her father warned. "The walls have ears. People still report on each other."

Meiling needed no warning about the neighbors. It was the same all over China. The nation's citizens had been forced into spying on each other and, for the sake of food or privileges, people were even willing to lie and exaggerate in the reports made to the authorities.

Meiling was intrigued with the padded closet where family members took turns listening to the Christian radio programs beamed into China.

"These programs have kept our faith alive," her mother explained one day. "One person listens inside the closet while others remain outside on guard. The leader reads a portion of Scripture slowly on each broadcast and that allows us to write it down. We have no Bibles except the handwritten ones we are making from these broadcasts. We have the Gospel of Mark and the Gospel of John written down already," her mother continued as she displayed the carefully written pages. "Oh, how precious is the Word of God!"

"Oh, I'd love to listen to a program," Meiling offered. "It has been years since I have heard any singing except the whispered songs in our night meetings. I am starved for the worship of a congregation of believers. The believers in Taiping are all so very poor that no one has been able to afford a radio. It would be such a great help if we did have one," she added thoughtfully.

At the appointed hour Meiling entered the closet with pen and paper, ready to take notes on the message but, most importantly, to record the Scripture that would be dictated.

"If anything unusual happens out here," Mrs. Woo explained, "we will give you a signal. Immediately turn off the radio and hide it in this secret place in the floor. Cover it with the rug and come out. We must always be vigilant so that our secret is not discovered. It is our only link with the outside world and with the Word of God."

That night the hymns broadcast on the radio touched Meiling's heart and brought tears of joy to her eyes. Not since the days before she was sent to the commune had she heard such beautiful singing. Memories of the joyful services they once enjoyed and of Pastor Yang flooded her mind, and with them came tender thoughts of Anching.

I wonder if he made it to safety in Hong Kong or Taiwan, she mused wistfully. *How many hundreds of times have I asked that question? I can never forget his last words to me as the army truck pulled away, but is it possible after all these years that we would meet again?*

Meiling was brought back to reality as the pastor began to speak.

"Thank You, precious Jesus!" she exulted quietly. "You have given me this privilege to hear a pastor expound Your Word and to hear Your people sing Your praises. Oh, how I wish the believers in Taiping could hear this heavenly message!" *I must try and buy a radio and take it back with me,* she thought, as she began to take notes on the message.

"It is time for the dictation of a chapter of the Bible," the announcer said. "Get your paper and pen ready. The reader will read one verse at a time very slowly, and then he will repeat it again. Are you ready? Here is our reader for today. He will read the wonderful, encouraging words of Psalm 103."

Meiling sat tense and eager to catch every word. She hadn't read Psalm 103 since before her Bible was burned by the Red Guards.

"Lord, thank You, she prayed, *"and bless Your Word so that we might grow because of it."*

The reader began.

"Psalm 103, verse one. 'Bless the Lord, O my soul…,'" he read slowly.

Meiling wrote the words down and rejoiced at the sound of them. The reader continued.

"'…and all that is within me….'" He paused as people all over China, hiding in closets like Meiling, were writing down God's Word. After a sufficient pause, the reader again continued.

"'…bless His holy Name.' Let me repeat verse one again," the reader said.

Meiling looked at her paper and read the words with the reader.

"Oh, how wonderful!" she exclaimed with joy.

"Verse two," the reader said. "'Bless the Lord, oh my soul…,'" and he paused again, as she feverishly wrote the precious words.

Again the voice took up the reading, "'And forget not all His benefits…,'" he read.

Meiling's heart raced at those beautiful words, *Surely the Lord has been good to me,* she mused, as the reader repeated the words of verse two again.

On and on he read, as Meiling carefully wrote each word, until the chapter was almost complete.

"Verse nineteen…," the voice read. "'The Lord has established His throne in heaven….'"

Meiling wrote, but as the reader read something tingled in her heart and mind. *That voice,* she thought. *I've heard that voice before! Who is reading this chapter?* she questioned, as she tried to keep writing.

"That voice," she said aloud. "I know that voice! It's Anching!" With unrestrained abandon she called out, "Anching is reading this chapter!"

Mrs. Woo, sitting outside of the closet, heard Meiling's excited voice. *Why is she talking in such a loud voice? It is too loud for safety!* she thought as she rose and hastily opened the door a crack.

"Meiling, what's going on? Stop talking so loudly!"

"Mother!" she called out as softly as possible in her excitement. "Mother, I think the Bible reader is Anching! Listen. Isn't that him?" she asked, trying desperately to believe. For the moment Mrs. Woo also forgot about security as she opened the door a little wider and listened carefully while the reader read the chapter again.

"I think it is Anching's voice," she agreed excitedly, as they both concentrated on the reader's voice. He finished reading the chapter and then signed off with a blessing.

"May the God who watches over us continually keep you safe in His wonderful care. Good night, and God bless you."

Hearing the commotion, Meiling's sister, who was home at the time, came over to see what was going on.

"We just heard Anching reading Psalm 103," exclaimed Meiling, trying to comprehend the startling fact. "He is alive. Oh, thank God, he is alive! He made it to Hong Kong! He's alive!" she said, as she danced around the room. And now he is broadcasting from there and helping us to restore our Bibles," she continued excitedly.

"*Ssshhh…,*" cautioned Mrs. Woo. "Not so loud, Meiling. Everyone in the apartment will hear you."

"How can you be so sure?" asked her sister doubtfully. "It's been more than twelve years since he left here. Did he announce his name?"

"No, but I would know his voice anywhere. Oh. Mother, he's alive! He's alive!"

There was no sleeping for Meiling that night. Long after she retired, her heart was singing a song of praise.

"I heard his voice," she kept saying over and over again. "He's alive! He's alive! Oh, praise You, Jesus. He's alive."

The next day she made her way over to Anching's home to give his family the good news.

"But we must not spread this word around, lest it reach the ears of some spy and they report us for having a radio," warned Meiling.

Chapter 7

THE LETTER

The month in Puyang had sped by rapidly for Meiling and her family, often with long talks late into the night. Now, as she sat on the train returning to Taiping, she wondered more than ever how she could contact Anching. Postal service with the outside world had long ago been cut off and the prospects of the resumption of service seemed even more remote as the chaos of the Red Guards continued.

Then, unexpectedly one day several weeks later in Puyang, the postman handed Mrs. Woo a letter with a flourish. "This is your lucky day," he said. "You are the first people on my route to receive a letter from Indonesia! It is addressed to your former residence of many years ago, but a worker in the post office recognized your name and knew where you were living. That was very fortunate because no one else knew anything about you."

"Oh, thank you," she exclaimed in surprise. "We don't know anyone in Indonesia!"

"Well, it's your lucky day all right," he repeated. "I hope it brings you lots of good luck. Maybe it brings you news of a big fortune you have inherited," he said with a chuckle. "You and I could both use that, don't you think?"

Mrs. Woo had suffered so much during these past fifteen years since the Communists had taken over that she was extremely cautious with every response to those outside her family. She just smiled and took the letter with a courteous, "Thank you."

"My family just received a letter from a friend in Indonesia, who had forwarded a letter from my uncle. We all thought he had died years ago in that last battle," the postman tried again.

Clutching her letter tightly, she replied simply, "I'm so glad to hear that." Then, turning quickly, she entered her home and closed the door securely behind her. With trembling hands she tore open the letter and scanned it quickly. Then she shouted with delight—throwing all caution to the wind as she called her husband.

"Come quick. Here's a letter from Anching!"

"What?" he exclaimed, as he hastily took the letter she offered him. Trembling with excitement she sat down in a chair as her husband read aloud.

"I hope and pray that somehow God will direct this letter to you, even though I am using your former address when you were the principal of our high school. I've heard recently that letters could be sent from Indonesia to China, and so I have asked an acquaintance there to forward this letter to you. At the end of the war, I escaped to Hong Kong, where I worked in a Christian hospital. Now I serve as assistant to the pastor in our church here. I have never forgotten my promise to Meiling to find her again some day. Maybe God will direct this letter to you and someone can help me in my search."

Mr. Woo felt faint as he sat down next to his wife. "I can hardly believe that after all these years we have heard from him again," he said with relief. "Surely the hand of the Lord has guided this letter to us."

For the next hour they read and talked about all the news the letter contained.

"We must write back immediately," Mr. Woo said, "and we must send this letter to Meiling. She will be overjoyed to hear from him at last. Oh, praise the Lord, for His goodness to all of us! Surely He is Victor—in spite of all that Satan has done to us."

It took another three weeks for the letter to reach Meiling in Taiping. That very day she sent a reply through the contact in Indonesia, and then she waited for an answer from Anching. Seven long, interminable months passed and still there was no reply, but daily she prayed for the impossible to happen.

"Lord, she prayed again and again, You're the God of the impossible. Work a miracle! You wrote the book on impossible things, and I believe your Word. I have waited all these years for some word that Anching is alive. You have answered that prayer, and I believe that You will answer this one."

Each time she prayed there was a serene sense of peace that flooded her heart, and she went on her way singing and waiting.

Returning to the church office one day, Anching was in high spirits. Another family in Rennie's Mill had achieved the goal of building a small cement block home that could withstand typhoons and fire. One of the delights of his heart was to celebrate a tradition among the believers of dedicating their homes to the glory of God.

"Lord," he prayed as he walked along, "what a perfect day for another answer to prayer! It's been almost a year since I sent that letter to the Woos. I know it seems absolutely impossible that after more than fifteen years a letter addressed to their old home in Puyang *should even reach them. I don't know if they're alive or even in the city anymore, but I'm trusting You for an answer."*

"Anching," called out Mrs. Sung from the doorway of her little home. "Anching, hurry! Here's a letter addressed to you from Indonesia!"

He fairly leaped forward with excitement and, taking the letter, hastily tore it open. *This may be my answer!* he thought, as he unfolded the letter with trembling hands. And then (with a whoop that could be heard all over the church area), he shouted. "It's from Meiling!"

Suddenly the turmoil and uncertainty of wondering if he would ever see her again—of hoping against hope that she was still alive—came to an end! Her letter had arrived, and he knew that she not only had survived the terrible years of suffering, but that she had also not forgotten him. In an instant he knew that his life, like the church in China, though shattered, was not lost; his hopes delayed, but not destroyed.

The Sungs and several friends gathered around to enjoy this thrilling moment of joy with Anching, who against all hope stood firm in his resolve to honor his promise, made so many years ago. As the excitement died down, he excused himself in order to read the letter again privately. Later, looking joyfully at his friends, he shocked them all with his words.

"Friends, I'm going to start making preparations to return to China as soon as possible!"

"That's impossible," said Mrs. Sung immediately.

"There's no way you could return," said another. "The country is in turmoil with the Red Guards in power. They're wrecking havoc everywhere. It would be too dangerous to return."

They all regarded Anching and his stated plan with great concern, thinking of every conceivable hardship that he would face.

"My dear friends, there is nothing too hard for God. He specializes in impossibilities. I must keep my promise to Meiling!"

Friends continued to plead with him to give up his plan to return to China. Even Pastor Sung urged him to be patient and to wait.

"China is in an uproar and chaos prevails all over the land. It is insane for a Christian and an ex-soldier to return to China at this time," he said over and over again with as much persuasion as possible. "You know how much I love you and need you in the work here," he pressed. "Anching, think of a lifetime of work for God that might be cut short and land you in prison for years. You will be walking into the lion's den!"

Nevertheless, one night after a week of fasting and prayer, Anching stood before the student body of the Bible School and shared the assurance that God had given him about returning.

"I thank you all for your prayers and your concern for my welfare but, dear friends, I can do nothing less than obey my Lord and follow where He leads. First of all, God has given me a special promise from Exodus 34:30 that assures me that He is leading me back to China. Here's what it says: "I will do wonders never before done in any nation in all the world. The people you live among will see how awesome is the work that I the Lord will do for you" (Exodus 34:10).

Every eye was riveted on him as he spoke. Each was examining their own heart as the words of this man, who was determined to follow Jesus no matter what the cost, impacted them. Some thought, *He's being carried away with a martyr complex. It's very foolish to even talk about returning to China at this point in time.* Others were moved by his devotion but frightened at the implications of his possible death.

"Lord," some prayed silently, *"is that what you expect me to do, also?"* Still others thought, *"God will use this man to stir China and bring many to salvation."* Everyone was occupied with his own thoughts when suddenly they heard Anching say something that startled them even more.

"Friends, I am moving out in faith, based on this promise from God. I love Jesus with all my heart, and I have proven Him to be trustworthy in all kinds of dangerous situations. I believe that when God calls, He enables. Recently I read something a brother in Christ who has suffered much for the cause of Jesus Christ said that moved my heart. He said: 'If you haven't found something you are willing to die for, you haven't discovered anything worth living for.'"

Everyone in the room was stunned by the statement. Not a sound could be heard anywhere, except the solemn words of this dedicated man of God.

"Friends, I am willing to die for Jesus. This week I placed my fondest dream of meeting my friend Meiling once again at the foot of the cross. I've determined that I must return to reach China for Christ's sake, even if I never find her. I must return because I love my countrymen and want them to discover the joy of knowing and serving Jesus."

Sensing the unusually strong Presence of the Holy Spirit in the room, Pastor Sung called for those who were willing to lay down their lives for Jesus to gather around Anching and pledge together to follow Jesus no matter where He led. It was an unforgettable night, as dozens pressed in close and laid their hands on him and pledged that they, too, would follow Jesus to the ends of the earth. A new vision for China was born in their hearts that night—and not for China only, but for the whole world.

The postal channel through Indonesia was slow, but effective. Meiling's heart leaped for joy as she read the first letter from Anching she'd received after a silence of more than eighteen years. She sat alone in her humble room and read his words, with tears flowing freely as he recounted his escape and eventual arrival in Hong Kong. Most of all, she was impressed by his firm commitment to serve God.

He hasn't changed a bit, she thought. *He is still the same dedicated man I knew so many years ago.* She was moved with deep emotion by the repetition of his promise to find her, even if it took the rest of his life.

"Thank You, Jesus. It has been very difficult waiting all these years for the fulfillment of his promise, but now I know it will some day be fulfilled."

Meiling and her friend, Yo, had visited together frequently ever since the day Anching's picture was discovered in the heap of debris on the floor of her hut.

"I am so thrilled over this news," she said, as Meiling shared her great joy, "and I'm so excited that I too will have the joy of meeting him once again."

"I don't know how it will be possible for us to meet again," Meiling confessed with a tinge of sadness in her voice, "but I believe the God who worked the miracle of this letter will work another one and bring us together again."

The train to the China border at Lowu in Hong Kong moved slowly out of the station. Anching's one small bag contained all of his earthly possessions, including his Bible. Several warned him not to take it, fearing that it would prevent him from entering China.

"It is the most precious possession I have. To leave it behind would be like leaving my closest friend. It is the source of strength that I must have to serve the Lord. He will get it through somehow," he said.

Yet in his heart, fear rose to new heights as he boarded the train. His mind said, *Turn back before it is too late,* but his heart compelled him to go on, knowing that the formidable obstacles before him were all under God's control.

"*Jesus,*" he prayed silently, "*I am moving out at your bidding. The obstacles are as great as the wall of Jericho that the Israelites faced when they crossed the Jordon River. You are my strength and my refuge; my only hope in every situation. I fully trust You and will not turn back.*"

Disembarking from the train at the China border, Anching walked across the Lowu Bridge, as all passengers are required to do. As he walked, he prayed that he would be directed to an accommodating official who would grant him the necessary travel documents. When his turn came, a stern-faced, middle-aged man motioned for him to come to his table and present his papers. Anching breathed a prayer, stepped up to the table, and handed the man his documents, with a request to enter China. The man perused the papers for a few moments and then, glancing up at Anching with a quizzical look on his face, questioned him.

"Do I understand that you are applying for permission to return to China to visit your parents in Wuhan?"

"Yes, sir," he responded, politely giving the man a broad smile.

"That's impossible. Only people on official business may enter China at this time," he said curtly.

"But, sir, my mother and father are growing very old, and I am the eldest son in the family. You understand Chinese custom and my obligations to the family."

"I told you only people on official business may enter at this time. Here, take your papers and move on. There are people waiting behind you, so don't waste their time."

"Sir," he persisted, "I was informed by reliable sources that our Chinese government honors elderly people who are good citizens and expects the eldest son to care for his parents so that they do not become a burden to the State. I am only trying to fulfill my obligations to my parents and to my country," he said disarmingly. "Isn't that what you would do for your parents?" he added.

"Young man," he responded with a softening attitude, "You sound much like my eldest son, who was killed in the revolution. It was one of the saddest days of my life when I heard that news. It is indeed a terrible thing not to enjoy the comfort of your eldest son," he said wistfully. Then, as an afterthought, he added, "But it would be useless for me to grant you travel documents because it would only be good as far as Canton, (known as *Guangzhou* today). You would have to apply in Canton for permission to make the next part of the journey to Wuhan—and I can guarantee you that it would not be granted."

"Please, sir," Anching replied with his contagious smile, "I would be delighted to accept your offer as far as Canton. Please, let me go as far as I can."

"Don't you realize that if your request is denied there that you would have a very difficult time returning to Hong Kong?" he replied, thinking he had placed an unacceptable obstacle in his path. Anching prayed silently for the right response to the agent, who seemed to be wavering.

"Sir," he said, looking the man straight in the eye, "my greatest desire is to see my parents again and to serve my country."

The man hesitated; Anching prayed earnestly. Without another word he stamped the documents with an entry permit and handed them back. As he did so, he motioned him through the gate, without even looking in his travel bag.

"Thank You, Jesus," he murmured. *"Thank You for this permission and for protecting my Bible! Surely this is an indication that You are leading me. Thank You for being my stronghold and my refuge."*

Stepping up to the ticket window, Anching purchased a third-class ticket to Canton—the cheapest form of transportation. Settling himself by a window, he prepared for the four-hour train run to Canton, trusting that God would overcome all obstacles in the next difficult circumstance he would soon face.

Chapter 8

A VISION IS BORN

s Pastor Yang arrived at the stone quarry prison, where he would fulfill his twenty-year sentence of "reeducation," he understood clearly that the sentence would quickly be reduced the moment he acquiesced to the government's demands and recanted his profession of faith. As he was stripped of all his possessions and the door to his cellblock clanged shut with a deafening clatter, he stood for a moment and looked around the sparsely furnished surroundings.

Twenty years, he thought. *How long will twenty years be in this place where people are treated like animals and deprived of all human decency?*

"Lord," he prayed sincerely, *"I am here at Your bidding. Help me to be Your man in this prison. Give me the strength and wisdom I will need to lead many to You. May Your church grow in this inhospitable place of sorrow and death so that Your Name will be glorified...."*

The next morning Pastor Yang ate his breakfast of thin rice gruel and marched off to the quarry, where hundreds of slave laborers chipped rocks all day long in a constant struggle to fulfill their daily quota by the end of the long day. That first night, fighting fatigue from the long day's work, he slumped down and silently ate his bowl of rice and vegetables. Once a month, he was told, there might be a small piece of meat or fish, but at best the diet was always insufficient to nourish bodies for the strenuous work they were required to do. Gradually, he became accustomed to the rigorous work of breaking up stones and then carrying the heavy buckets to the counting bin.

I do not have to finish my prison term, but I must never waiver in my faith. I must live for Jesus in this place of darkness and bring as many as possible with me to heaven.

Soon his reputation spread throughout the camp as dozens of men sought him out for spiritual help and comfort. In spite of threats and privation, the authorities were not able to keep men from seeking out "the pastor" for spiritual help. It was a one-on-one ministry that exceeded his wildest imagination, even though there never was an opportunity to meet as a group in formal worship. Men learned Scripture passages and hymns, and how to pray, all from one man who loved Jesus with all his heart.

One day as the workers marched out to the quarry pits a former landowner, who had once enjoyed succulent food every day, struggled to keep up with the others. Risking a blow in the ribs from the butt of a rifle, Pastor Yang whispered encouragement to him to help him keep up with the others. To fall behind brought a severe beating from the guards, and on occasion they even shot stragglers on the spot.

The two of them had worked together several times recently and, when opportunity presented itself, Pastor Yang shared a few words of the hope he had in Christ with this man. Prisoners always enjoyed working with him, because even a few words of encouragement lifted their spirits and helped them through another difficult day. Helping others in need was risky business indeed, but Pastor Yang believed that he was in this prison by God's appointment, in order to help men find their way to God.

As the two men walked along in the brisk morning breeze, the man fell to grumbling about the cold and the thin garments provided that were little protection from the weather.

"Better speak more softly," Pastor Yang whispered. "The guards may hear you."

"I don't care if they do," he replied much too loudly for safety's sake. "They're animals, and I've had enough!"

A guard nearby shouted at him to be quiet and move along faster, and to emphasize his command he jabbed his rifle butt violently into his side. The force of the blow took his breath away and caused him to stop, bowed over with pain. Rushing forward, the guard shouted at him to get moving and, grabbing him by the shoulder, shoved him forward so violently that he lost his balance, stumbled, and fell to the ground. Standing over the poor man, the guard rained blow after blow on his defenseless body with his rifle butt.

Instinctively, Pastor Yang threw himself over the man to protect him from the vicious beating. The guard screamed in fury as he struck Pastor Yang on the back, blow upon blow.

"Get up and get back in line, or I'll shoot!"

"Please," Pastor Yang implored, as he struggled to his feet. "Please don't hit him again. I'll take responsibility to see that he gets in line and keeps up with the rest of the men. Please don't hit him again."

Stunned by the pastor's actions, the surprised guard stood there for a moment, uncertain what to do.

"Please," Pastor Yang pleaded again, as he noticed the guard's uncertainty. "Let us catch up with the rest." As he said this, he pulled the man to his feet and urged him to start walking. The guard, still shocked by a prisoner taking another's beating, allowed them to start walking again toward the quarry.

Pastor Yang draped the man's arm over his shoulder and hurried him along as he whispered to him, "Just keep walking, or they'll beat you to death."

When they reached the quarry Pastor Yang pulled the man down by a pile of rocks. "Start working," he ordered. "Don't let them think you are injured. I'll help you get your quota today, but just work as fast as you can."

The man nodded his understanding and started crushing his pile of rock. Obviously he was injured from the beating and weakened from long months of starvation, but he did as Pastor Yang urged him. There was no opportunity for conversation as the angry guard stood close by, watching for any infraction that would allow him to vent his anger on the man. Eventually, as the guard moved on, the man looked over at the pastor and spoke to him in a soft voice, "Why did you stop the guard from beating me? I have nothing left to live for. Death would have been most welcome."

"But you do have lots to live for," admonished the pastor. "You have a wife and family, don't you? Some day you will be freed from this awful place, and you will be reunited with them. Isn't that worth living for? Never give up hope," he whispered, as he looked around to see where the guards were.

"What hope does a man have in a place like this? They weaken us by starvation, and then beat us when we don't have the strength to make the day's quota. Life is hopeless. I want to die."

"But if you die, where will you go?"

"Death itself will be release enough to end my misery."

"Ah, my bother," replied Pastor Yang, as he pounded away at his pile of rocks. "Death is not the end. There is life beyond the grave. For me, I have eternal life because I have trusted in Jesus as my Savior. He has forgiven me of all my sin and given me the hope of eternal life." Seeing the guard approaching, he whispered quickly, "Here comes the guard. Work harder."

Both men ceased speaking and worked hard at filling their bucket. Their quota was forty buckets a day, rain or shine, in heat or cold, summer or winter—it never varied. Pastor Yang had filled three buckets already; his friend had only half a bucket.

"Get busy, old man," the guard called out gruffly, looking at the half-filled bucket. "You're way behind with your quota. They'll be another beating for you if you fail to make your quota. And your friend here won't be there to take it for you next time," he said, with a sinister sneer on his face.

As the guard strolled on, Pastor Yang scooped up some crushed rocks and added them to his friend's bucket. He would have to work much faster to help him get his quota. There were no shovels to use, just their bare hands. After years of scooping up the crushed rocks with his bare hands in the bitter wind of winter and the sweltering heat of summer, Pastor Yang's hands had become calloused and rough.

Gazing ruefully at his hands, he thought, *These once could write beautiful Chinese characters on scrolls, and people vied for the privilege of owning one of my Scripture mottos. I doubt if they could even hold a brush any longer....*

His thoughts were interrupted by his friend's question. "Why are you doing this for me?"

"Because I want you to know that Jesus loves you and died in your place on the cross to save you."

"Is that why you covered me with your own body and took my beating this morning?" he asked unexpectedly. "I've been thinking about that. Why would you take my beating?"

"Keep working and I'll tell you," responded Pastor Yang, as a song of praise rose in his heart. He prayed daily for God to open men's hearts through his actions and words of encouragement so that he could have the opportunity of leading them to Jesus. He worked faster than usual to fill his bucket, while helping his suffering friend with a scoop now and then as he kept strict watch over the movements of the guards. When opportunity to speak a few words was possible, he shared the gospel story and answered the man's questions.

"Now I'm beginning to understand why you took my beating," he said late in the afternoon. "You did what Jesus did for you and me when He died on the cross. He took our beatings, didn't He?"

"That's right, and just as you accepted my gift to you this morning, so Jesus wants you to accept His gift of eternal life."

From a Source outside of himself, Pastor Yang had the strength to reach his quota an hour before quitting time. *"Thank You, Jesus, for the strength You are giving me today to demonstrate Your love to this man. Open his heart and reveal Yourself to him, and give me the strength to help him reach his quota of rock today."*

"I'm not going to make my quota," lamented the man. "I'm only on number thirty-one so far."

Don't worry. I will help you. I've finished my quota already. Now we'll work together on yours."

"Pastor Yang, you are the most remarkable man I have ever met," said the man, as he paused in his work. "I doubt if there is another prisoner in all of China who would do what you are doing for me."

"Brother, I am only doing what Jesus would do. Now, let's get back to work or you will get a beating tonight."

Half-an-hour later the man groaned as the whistle blew shrilly, announcing that there were only thirty minutes left before quitting time.

"I've still got to fill three more buckets," he said in despair. "I don't think I can make it."

"Just keep working," urged the pastor. "We'll get it done."

Working feverishly to help his friend, Pastor Yang's hands throbbed with pain.

"Lord, help us," he prayed. A few minutes before the final whistle blew the man staggered to the counting bin, dumping in his last

bucket! Pastor Yang stood erect and stretched his back as a song of praise flooded his heart.

"You helped us, Lord!" he exulted. *"You helped us make the quota! Oh, praise Your wonderful, holy Name! Please let my friend know that it was You who enabled us to do it."*

The guard came by to check the accounts. He looked at the man in amazement for a long moment, and then he spoke. "You made your quota, I see. How did you do that? The last time I checked on you, you were far behind."

The man just stood quietly by, but his heart was overflowing with joy. *"God,"* he prayed, *"now I know You are real. You really helped me today through Pastor Yang."*

"I don't know how you did it," the guard said, as he walked away with a puzzled look on his face. "But I warn you, don't try any more of your tricks—like you did this morning—or I'll finish you and that pastor off next time."

"I don't know how he did it," he remarked to another guard. "I gave him a beating this morning that should have laid him up for a week, and yet he still made the quota! I'll bet that pastor helped him somehow. He is an amazing man!"

"And I noticed that he took a lot of that man's beating this morning."

"He did, and I don't know why. Life is hard enough to bear here, even for us," the guard said, "and I sure don't know why anyone would take another man's beating!"

"I've seen the pastor do things like that for the others, too," said his fellow guard. "Do you think it has anything to do with that foreign religion he believes in?"

"I don't have any idea, but from now on I'm going to watch him and find out."

A few weeks later, on a cold windy day with a hint of snow in the air, the prisoners were marched out to the quarry after only a bowl of thin gruel for breakfast. The dark, threatening sky added to the depressing conditions of the camp as the cold, hungry men struggled to meet their quota of chipped rock. As always, Pastor Yang hunched over his pile of large rocks, hammering away to crush them into smaller pieces to fill his bucket and meet his quota. His heart seemed as heavy as the dark, ominous clouds that shrouded the mountaintop above the quarry, hiding it from view. *How many times I have looked up at that mountain,* he thought, *and quoted Psalm 121: "I lift up my eyes to the hills—where does my help come from? My help comes from the Lord, the maker of heaven and earth"* (Psalm 121:1).

On this particular day, with heavy heart, he thought back to the comfortable home he had enjoyed before being imprisoned here. He remembered his loving wife, who had worked by his side in the church. Now she struggled daily to make ends meet. Expelled from their little home at the church, she was forced to work in a factory for a pittance, supplying products for export to nations around the world.

The people purchasing those products don't realize that people who are little more than slaves held bondage by a ruthless government made them, he thought in despair. *The church is closed and the people scattered. Who is caring for their souls? The iron grip of the Communist government tightens around their necks! Their Bibles are gone! "Oh, Lord, how will they survive?"* he prayed.

Depression swept over him like great ocean waves as the fierce blows of Satan's attacks struck him like sharp arrows. He looked to the mountain and cried out to the Lord for help and deliverance.

"Lord," he cried as he hammered away at his pile of rocks, *"for many years I have sought to follow You. I thought when You sent me to Puyang several years ago that You would use me there to reach many people with the gospel, but now, look at me,"* he moaned. *"I'm a prisoner in this miserable place, able only to whisper to men about You. I thought You had bigger things in mind for me. The church was growing and beginning to reach out to hundreds of people. Now my every movement is restricted; my body is tormented by hunger and cold but, worst of all, I can do so little for Your Kingdom. You called me to preach the good news, but instead I crush stones all day long."*

It seemed like God was far away and that his prayers bounced off the dark clouds that hung over the quarry. Hot tears ran down his cheeks, falling on the rocks he was crushing.

These rocks are just like my heart, he thought, *crushed and broken. I've been here only a few of the twenty years I must fulfill, but already it seems like eternity. How can I endure the years of my sentence and keep my sanity? How will I be able to fulfill my calling with this hammer and bucket?*

"That's easy," a soothing voice spoke in his ear. "Just tell the authorities that you are ready to give up the false notion that Jesus will help you in this prison. Tell them that you will work for them. Your wife could be so much more comfortable, and so could you, if you would only realize you can't stand up against this powerful government.

"And besides," continued the sugar-coated voice, "doesn't the Bible say that you should obey the authorities God has placed over you?"

Pastor Yang raised his hammer and slammed it down viciously on the rock before him. "Be gone, Satan!" he said vehemently. "You are a deceitful liar from the very beginning. I claim victory over you in the all-powerful Name of Jesus. I will not recant! I will never turn my back on my Savior! I will serve Him until my last breath, even in this prison!"

Again and again he pounded the rock and smashed it to bits. Looking up, he saw a break in the clouds—a little ray of sunlight was shining through the gloom. The wonderful peace of God suddenly flooded into his heart.

"Oh, Jesus, forgive me for the thoughts of despair that filled my heart," he cried. *"I know You are here in this place and You planted me here for a purpose. I will not turn back. I am Yours for eternity...."*
A song welled up in his heart and he sang softly to himself:

Though the whole world hates me, and friends forsake me,
Though my fleshly temple be destroyed by slander, persecution, and beatings,
I will give my life and spill my blood to please my Heavenly Father,
That, wearing the crown of life, I will enter the Kingdom of God.

(Composed by Pastor Yun, The Heavenly Man)

The last syllable was still on Pastor Yang's lips when He heard the voice of Jesus in his heart. *"My son, I love you and I am with you. Don't be afraid or discouraged. You are doing more for the Kingdom than crushing rocks. There are yet many in this prison who need to hear about the way of salvation, and I have chosen you to be My witness. But beyond that, I have other plans for you. One day you will leave this place, and you will begin a Bible School to train young people for ministry. They will travel far and wide to spread the gospel, and many will be saved. Prepare your heart to lead them by the lessons you are learning now."*
It was a hallowed moment on the rocky ground of the quarry. He felt like Moses standing on holy ground in the Presence of the Almighty. The vision was too big for him to comprehend—"...start a Bible School to prepare young people to spread the gospel!" Like Abraham looking at all the stars of the sky, he bowed in humble adoration and cried out, simply, *"Yes, Lord, I will obey."*
From that day forward Pastor Yang knew where he was headed. He began to pray for the young people who formerly worshipped in

the Puyang Church, mentioning Meiling and Anching in particular, as well as dozens more. The new vision burned in his heart.

"Lord, I believe," he sang. *"I believe."*

One day as he was working at his endless task of crushing rock, he heard a commotion. Looking up, he saw three ragged men pummeling the friend he had protected some weeks previous. He was on the ground, curled up in a fetal position with his hands over his head, attempting to protect himself from the blows the three were raining on him. While one continued to beat him up, the other two began gathering up his crushed stones, which had spilled from his bucket. Pastor Yang dropped his hammer and ran to help his friend.

"Stop," he yelled. "I saw you knock him down, and now you're stealing his crushed stones. You can't do that!"

The three men now turned and attacked him and, knocking him down to the ground, began kicking him in the stomach and groin. Two guards, who had been huddling around a small charcoal fire in the guardhouse, rushed out to break up the fight. Whips in hand, they swung them viciously at the men. One lash caught Pastor Yang across his shoulder and neck, breaking his skin and causing the blood to flow. The three thugs stumbled backwards as the blows of the whip found their mark and stung their hands and legs.

"What's going on here?" one of the guards shouted as he stood over the helpless man the three had knocked down.

"These two men," one of the ragged men whined, pointing to the bruised man sitting on the ground and Pastor Yang, "tried to steal my bucket of rocks. My friends here came to my rescue."

"That's a lie," shouted the man on the ground. These three men attacked me as I was heading toward the counting bin," he rasped, still winded from the beating he had received.

"Look, you can see that their three buckets are empty, and the rocks scattered here make up only one bucketful. Pastor Yang came to my rescue. He saved me from being killed."

A word battle ensued as the bewildered guards tried to sift through the arguments, not knowing whom to believe.

"I think I've seen you before," one of the guards said finally, looking at Pastor Yang. "Aren't you the one who took the other man's beating a few weeks ago?" he asked, with curiosity.

"Yes," he replied simply.

The guard turned and scrutinized the man on the ground. "And you're the same man I had to punish for failing to keep up with the other men. Isn't that right?" he asked.

"Yes, sir, that's right. But I was doing my work today when these men attacked me and tried to steal my crushed rocks."

"And so you're at it again, keeping this man from being beaten," the guard said, addressing Pastor Yang. "Who are you—the savior of all these men? What makes you get involved in their problems like this? You took his beating a few weeks ago and now you got cut with the whip. Why?" he asked, incredulously.

"Whenever you attempt to help someone, you run the risk of getting hurt," Pastor Yang replied. "I am a Christian pastor. I want to serve people in trouble and relieve some of their pain and suffering."

The young guard squirmed at this bold statement by a prisoner. "It isn't easy for us, either," he replied defensively. "Most of the prisoners are uncooperative. We are not bad people," he continued. "We're just carrying out our orders, and if we don't, we are punished. Did you know that?"

"I suspected that," Pastor Yang replied, sensing that the guard was telling more than his superiors would want him to reveal.

"OK, enough of this talk," spoke up the other guard standing nearby.

"You men," he said, pointing to the three who had attacked the older man, "we know this man goes about doing good here in this prison, and we believe his story. So, you men get busy, and each of you produce three extra buckets of rock above your quota by nightfall or you will not be given anything to eat tonight," he ordered sternly. "Now get back to work, and if you ever touch these men again, you'll be given a good beating that you will remember for a long time."

Glaring angrily at the older man still sitting on the ground, the three men slinked away. Pastor Yang helped the man to his feet and gathered up his rocks.

"Looks to me like your bucket is full again," he encouraged, with a smile. "Better take it over to the counting bin and get it registered."

"Oh, Pastor Yang, how can I ever thank you for all you have done for me?"

"Don't," he replied simply. "Just help someone else in this prison. That will be my pay."

The guards walked back to the guardhouse, shaking their heads in disbelief.

"We've just witnessed an unbelievable act of kindness by that pastor," one said. "Whatever God he serves must be very proud of him," he said, thoughtfully.

"You're right," the other replied. "This is the second encounter we've had with his good deeds. If he keeps it up, he'll change this place!"

Chapter 9

THE SURPRISE

Tension filled the air night and day as the government tightened its noose on the freedom of the people. Even family members were cautious in voicing their opinions in their own homes. All churches had now been closed and church meetings were strictly forbidden. So dangerous were the times that even secret meetings were very scarce, and many wondered how they could maintain their faith under such stressful circumstances. Even Meiling, who was very courageous and willing to risk her life for the people, found it necessary to restrict her movements and meetings with others. One day, however, she stepped out by faith in obedience to God's leading.

Waiting upon the Lord for direction, she was led to take a walk past the church. As she approached it, she noticed that several guards were pacing back and forth in front of the building, making certain that no one stopped or loitered in the area. While still some distance away, she was surprised when a dear sister in the Lord stepped out of her doorway and joined her for the walk.

"Pingan," she whispered, meaning "Peace," the typical Chinese Christian greeting.

"God is so good to send you along right now. I was feeling discouraged and downcast, but the Lord prompted me to go out for a walk. When I saw you coming, I knew you were God's answer to my prayer."

"I also was prompted by God to go for a walk today, Meiling responded warmly. "Now I know the reason, but be very careful as we pass the church. Do not look at the building or in the direction of the guards, and don't say anything until we are past them."

Watching the men out of the corner of her eye, Meiling observed them scrutinizing them carefully. The women walked quietly by without incident. Both were occupied with memories of their beloved church. Meiling's throat choked up as she remembered the many times she and Anching had listened to Pastor Yang preaching in the Puyang Church—challenging them to live for Jesus no matter what the circumstances!

Her mind drifted to thoughts of Anching. *But when will I see him again? What does he look like now? Oh, Jesus,* she prayed, *hasten the day when we can be together again.*

Safely past the guards, both women sighed in relief.

"Oh, Sister," the old woman asked, "did you feel the Presence of the Lord as we walked past our church?"

"Yes, I did," Meiling responded happily, "but, of course, you know that He is with us wherever we go. No one can take away His Presence from us; not even the whole Communist army!"

"True! And His Presence was so powerful; my heart is so refreshed!"

They continued on for a distance, quietly talking of the Lord and encouraging each other in the Word.

"I must leave now," the older woman said, as she firmly grasped Meiling's hand. "Thank you for helping me to focus on Jesus again. I can go on now, in spite of these evil men all around us."

With an inner urge to continue walking, Meiling approached the main police station, where Luping had manhandled her. She shuddered as she remembered the brutal blows she had suffered, but she rejoiced that those blows led to his mother becoming a believer.

"Keep walking," the inner voice prompted her, and she did. Suddenly a small child darted out from the building, ran up to her, handed her a piece of paper, then disappeared into the building as quickly as she had appeared. Puzzled, Meiling continued walking as if nothing unusual had happened. At a safe distance from the building, she opened the note and read: "You are being watched night and day. Be careful, and cease visiting people, or I cannot be responsible for you." It was signed: "A concerned friend."

The only person she knew in the police station was Luping. *Was he sending her a warning note?* Although she occasionally visited his mother, she never met him again.

"He has changed so much," his mother had said when she had last visited. "Somehow I believe God is changing his heart." Meiling pondered all these thoughts as she continued walking in a big circle back to her apartment.

"The times are more stressful and dangerous than ever, Lord. Guide my steps and help me be more careful. But, Lord, I am ready for whatever You allow, because I must continue to encourage Your people."

Several weeks passed by uneventfully as she remained closer to home than usual, but her flock was begging for a gathering, and so it was secretly arranged to meet in an isolated spot deep in the forest at the north end of town. One by one the people assembled in the darkness of the moonless night. They came with expectant hearts and searching souls. Just a few glimmers of light appeared in the inner circle, as bodies pressed closer together to hide the light used to read the few pages of the Bible they had assembled. The people hung on to every word Meiling shared with them and murmured a frequent "Amen" in agreement.

Just as the fifty or so people gathered in the close circle were about to leave, unexpectedly a beam of light broke through the darkness. They found themselves surrounded by a ring of bright flashlights, as police clubs began swinging mercilessly. People fell to the ground, stunned by the blows and frightened by the shouts and threats. No one had opportunity to escape, as more than one hundred and fifty police officers surrounded them. Pressing to the center and aiming their flashlights directly into faces, they sought out Meiling and the elders.

This was no ordinary raid. The police knew exactly who they were looking for. No doubt an informant had set them up, which was an ever-present danger. Most likely someone had infiltrated their ranks, professing to be a follower of Jesus but intent only on reaping some benefit from the police. They pressed right to the center of the group, grabbed Meiling roughly by the arms, pinning them behind her. They shoved her ahead of them toward the waiting police vans.

Elder Chu and other leaders were beaten with clubs as they stumbled toward the vans. Meiling screamed as the searing pain of an electric prod was suddenly thrust against her body. In the van, the prisoners' hands were freed momentarily only to be clamped to a rod on the roof of the van. The vans took off at breakneck speed as the standing prisoners attempted to steady themselves. Elder Chu started to sing! The others in the van joined him, in spite of the verbal threats of the police in the cab. Roaring through the darkened streets, the sound of music filled the air and Jesus was praised.

At the police station Meiling was separated from the others and prodded with the electric stick as she was pushed forward to a cell. Each time the stick touched her, searing pain coursed through her body, causing her to stumble and nearly fall. The cell door opened and she was violently shoved to the floor, as the door clanged shut. Bruised all over from the shock treatment, she lay on the cold floor, exhausted and unable to move.

Meiling was unaware how long she lay there but, finally regaining some strength, she crawled to the bamboo bed and stretched out, drifting into unconsciousness until daylight. Roused by a guard, she was again pushed forward, although this time not with an electric stick. Her hair was disheveled and her face bloodied as she entered an interrogation room, where a neatly dressed officer of high rank sat at his desk.

"How many times must you be warned to cease your Christian activities?" he bellowed threateningly. "Now tell me where you are obtaining those pages of the Bible, or you will be beaten severely." Meiling stood quietly, not uttering a word.

"Answer me," he shouted angrily. Still no response.

Grabbing an electric stick, he forced her to her knees and, sticking the end of the rod in her mouth, sent a shock through her mouth and head that made her dizzy with pain and caused spots of light to appear before her eyes. Her mouth burned so badly from the shock that she could not speak. The torture continued unabated until she despaired of her life, but still she refused to divulge any information about the sheets.

Between his shouting and her screams of pain every time the electric stick was thrust into her mouth, even the policemen standing nearby turned away from the ugly sight of this helpless victim. Suddenly the door opened and Chief Pang Luping entered. Walking quickly to the officer administering the punishing electric shock treatment, he ordered him to cease.

"Enough!" he ordered. "Send her back to her cell."

The officer, red-faced with anger, began to speak, but Luping cut him off.

"Do as I've ordered," he commanded. Reluctantly, he obeyed and ordered the guards to take her back to her cell. As the men left, an argument ensued and tempers rose.

"You may be Chief of Police," cried out the officer in a rage, "but you cannot harbor a Christian, no matter how beautiful she may be. You have not heard the last of this incident."

With that outburst, he stalked out of the room, leaving Luping alone.

Meiling lay exhausted on her hard bed, thankful that the Lord had sustained her during this horrible torture session. She also rejoiced that she had not revealed anything about the Bible sheets. About an hour had passed when the sound of a key turning in the cell lock aroused her, filling her heart with fear that more shock treatments were in store for her. A woman guard brought her a pan of water.

"Clean yourself up," she said simply. "You are being sent home."

Dazed, she painfully rose from her bed, washed her face, and straightened her hair as she wondered what miracle had saved her again. She painfully made her way home and dropped onto her bed, exhausted but relieved. Once again she focused on the one thought that always lifted her heart: "Jesus is Victor."

Three weeks passed before she had regained her strength. Feeling better, Meiling made her way to Mrs. Pang's home. She was surprised to find the old woman in tears.

"What is the matter, Sister Pang?"

"Oh, Meiling, I don't know whether to cry or laugh," she responded. "A few days ago, Luping and I had a long talk. He told me everything that happened to you, and how he had released you from the prison. I praised him for that and told him God would honor him for his kindness to you."

"He set me free?" Meiling exclaimed, joyfully.

"I asked him why he had set you free. He looked me straight in the eye and said, 'Mother, at last I have Meiling's courage to stand up for Jesus. I prayed to receive Him into my life, and I am ready now to stand in His Presence.' Meiling, I was so shocked I could scarcely believe my ears! He has been so rebellious all of his life, and so cruel to the Christians.

"We prayed together and he confessed Jesus as his Lord. My heart was overflowing with joy and thanksgiving. But Meiling, the police came here two nights ago and arrested him, carting him off in handcuffs. I have not heard from him since."

Meiling held the old woman in her arms to comfort her.

"He will always be safe in the arms of Jesus," she soothed.

Three days later, Mrs. Pang was informed that her son had died suddenly in prison from an unknown cause. She could come and pick up his body.

Chapter 10

THE MAN IN HIS DREAM

Knocking on the door of Pastor Hu's home in Canton, Anching waited in anticipation of his first contact in the city. The door opened a crack and a pale faced man peered out questioningly.

"Yes," he asked carefully, "how may I help you?" The two men had never met before.

"I am Wen Anching," he said quietly, as he handed the old pastor a letter Pastor Sung had written to his old friend. The pastor took the letter, excused himself, and closed the door.

"Please, wait a moment," he said. A few minutes passed as Anching waited patiently, praying that the pastor would accept Pastor Sung's letter as authentic. He was rewarded, as the door opened and he was invited inside.

"So you are a coworker of my dear friend, Pastor Sung," he said as he invited him to sit down. "Tell me about him. He has always been a fearless preacher of the gospel." For the next two hours the men conversed about Pastor Sung and his activities. Then, smiling broadly he confided in Anching.

"Now that we have talked, I believe you are a true believer and are truly recommended by Pastor Sung. One cannot be too careful these days. Not everyone that comes with a letter of recommendation is reliable. How sad that we must question everyone these days! I welcome you to my humble home for as long as you need a place to rest," he said with a disarming smile.

"My dear friend speaks very highly of you," he continued, "and informed me that you feel called by God to return to China to minister to His people. Young man, do you understand the cost of such a calling?"

Waiting for Anching to answer, he searched his face, himself knowing full well the cost. He had just been released four months ago from hard labor in a slave camp. He bore the marks of torture on his wrists and ankles from the chains that had bound him, and if Anching could have seen his back he would have seen the ugly scars of many beatings.

"I understand the cost of serving Jesus in Communist China, but I can do nothing else than give Him my life," Anching replied, soberly.

That evening they made their way to a secret meeting place, where Anching spoke to the people of his decision to brave the lion's den to preach the gospel.

"Bless you, young man," an old woman spoke up. "It will not be easy. It will be the most costly decision you have ever made, but Jesus will see you through," she added prophetically.

During the days ahead the little flock of believers discovered both how deeply Anching felt about his calling and how effective he was in opening the Word to them. They also learned of his search for Meiling, and they prayed earnestly for him.

A restlessness gripped Anching's heart as he waited for God's leading concerning his journey to Taiping to search for Meiling. Strangely, his travel documents did not specify his destination. Pastor Hu examined the papers carefully and, looking at Anching in amazement, he concluded that God was in this.

"Anching, for some reason your papers do not indicate your destination. It looks like an oversight by the border official. I believe this is both good and bad news. Good, because you will not be breaking the law by going outside the area indicated in your papers, but bad if you should be apprehended in a secret meeting and interrogated by a burly police officer. He could make a case out of this, I am sure. They are masters at that."

"I have thought of that myself," Anching answered, "but I believe God has had control over my papers being as they are, so I do not need to go to the police for permission to travel. I can honestly say I am ignorant of the reason that no area is indicated. I will trust the Lord to take care of me in those circumstances."

"True," replied the pastor, "but you must be careful. I believe you must always tell the authorities that you are bound for Puyang to visit your parents, as it states here in this document. Be careful to be consistent in your statements. You ultimately hope to find Meiling, but you must leave that in God's hands. Follow where He leads, even if God leads you off on a tangent and you're delayed along the way. God has a perfect plan for you, and in His time and way He will unite you with Meiling."

"Thank you, pastor, for that good advice. Yes, I am impatient to find Meiling now that I am in China, but I understand the perils I am facing. I will try and be patient and to follow as God leads me."

That night as he lay on his bed meditating on the promises of God, Anching slipped into a peaceful sleep. Several hours later, he awakened with the realization that God had revealed his next step. In his dream he had seen a man from a distant area standing by his bedside, calling him by name.

"Wen Anching, I have been sent by God to invite you to my home, where my family is waiting to hear the gospel. You are to come with me, for many people are waiting to find the way to God. Tomorrow at about 3 P.M. I will come to Pastor Hu's home. You will know I have been sent from God to guide you to my home because I will bring a sheet of paper that has the most beautiful words I have ever read written upon it. I do not know who wrote the words or what book it is from, but my family wants you to come and explain the meaning of these words to them."

Anching lay awake for a long time, pondering the dream.

Could it be true that God had revealed his next step to him? Would a man really appear with a mysterious sheet of paper? A warm sense of God's Presence filled the room, bringing peace to his heart.

"I will follow wherever You lead me, Lord," he breathed in prayer.

In the morning he shared the dream with Pastor Hu.

"I have been praying for God to show me the way," he confessed. "I must move on, but I want only to move in God's direction."

"My son," the pastor replied, with an understanding nod of his head, "should such a man arrive today, you will know that God is leading you. Let's wait and see what God will do."

Two or three people slipped into the pastor's home in the early afternoon and listened intently as Anching opened the Word.

"This young man has an unusual anointing on him," explained the pastor. "He shares the Word with keen insights that have blessed my old heart. I believe he is destined to be a mighty instrument in God's hands."

All thought of time was forgotten as the small group of listeners huddled around the Word. When a knock came at the door it startled them, and they waited apprehensively. Every knock in China was met with trepidation, for one could never know when the police might show up at the door. A few moments later, Pastor Hu appeared with a man who was obviously a farmer by his dress.

Inviting him to sit in the circle, Pastor Hu looked at Anching and spoke.

"Here is the man of your dream!"

The people in the circle looked at the pastor, questioning what he meant.

The man sat on the edge of the chair and reached into his pocket as he spoke.

"Someone in brilliant white appeared to me in a dream three nights ago and said to me that I should come to this address and there I would find a man by the name of Wen Anching. I was told that he would come with me and would explain the sheet of paper that I found with the most beautiful words I have ever read. This person in shining white garments told me that the man was a choice servant of God and that he would bring the message of light and salvation to my family. Here is the paper. Now tell me, who is Wen Anching?" he asked, searching the faces of the men in the group.

Anching sat stunned for a moment.

This is exactly what my dream revealed—a man would come to Pastor Hu's home with a sheet of paper and ask me to go with him and tell his family about the way of salvation!

"My name is Wen," he replied, as he took the proffered sheet of paper. Perusing it quickly, he recognized its meaning. It was a partial, handwritten page of the third chapter of the Gospel of John; the story of Nicodemus, who came to Jesus seeking the way to God.

"This is a portion of the Bible," said Anching. "Where did you get this?"

"I was walking along the road near my home a few weeks ago when suddenly a strong breeze blew in out of nowhere, and this sheet of paper came floating through the air. I read it several times, trying to understand its meaning. I read it to my wife and my family, but the story is not complete. We want to know the rest of the story. Can you help us?"

"I certainly can. My Bible has the entire story of this man's search for God," he said.

"Then, will you come with me today? My family is waiting to hear the story."

"God also spoke to me in a dream last night and revealed to me that a man with a sheet of paper in his hand would come here to Pastor Hu's home at about 3 P.M. today. Everything is as it was in my dream. Yes, I am ready to go with you now."

Jumping up, the man clapped his hands with excitement.

"Then hurry; there is just enough time for us to catch the next bus to my home."

"Anching," spoke up Pastor Hu, "this is clearly a direction from God. It will be dangerous and you must be careful. Constantly listen to God's instruction from His Word and speak boldly the message of salvation. The Lord be with you."

A few minutes later Anching bid the Pastor farewell and began a journey into the unknown with his new friend and with God. It was after 8 P.M. when they finally arrived at their destination in a remote area.

As they got off the bus, the farmer turned to Anching and said, "I have two bicycles here for the rest of the journey. It is still about ten miles to my home, but the moon will soon be out and we will be able to see quite easily. My family is waiting to hear the explanation of this page. My elderly mother urged me to find you. She said she doesn't have much time left in this world, and she is afraid of dying."

"Let's go," replied Anching, though weary in body from the rough bus ride.

By 10 P.M. they arrived at the outskirts of the rural mountain town, and a few minutes later they pulled up in front of a small house. The oil lamps gave a faint glow that made it impossible to distinguish faces very easily. The room was filled with about twenty people, who gave a warm welcome to Anching as he was introduced to them.

"Wife," called the man, "prepare some food for our guest. He has not eaten since noon. Now come with me and meet my old mother," he said, as he led the way to another room with a small oil lamp on the wall.

"This is my mother, who is seeking the way to God," he stated simply by way of introduction.

"Mother, this is the man who can tell us the rest of the story about God."

Kneeling beside her bed, Anching took her hand in his, and gently stroked it. The touch of her frail fingers brought a flood of memories of his own mother. How he longed to see her again. *Would that day ever come?* he wondered. There was little time for contemplation about his family and Meiling as the old woman began to speak in little more than whispered tones.

"Tell me quickly," she began, "I have been searching for the way of salvation all my life, but now I am nearing the end of the journey. I have faithfully followed the gods of China. Every feast day has been observed, and offerings of food have been placed before the altar. I have not neglected the ancestors, not even once, and daily I have burned incense at the altar to the gods, but there has never been any response in my heart.

"Worse than that," she continued, "the road I am traveling on has come to an end at a great precipice. On the other side of the great divide, I can faintly see a light shining. It fills my heart with warmth when I look at it, but I see no way to cross this great divide. The road ends at the precipice, and other travelers on this same road are being pushed over the cliff by the press of the crowd. And I am being pushed forward, too. Tell me, is there no bridge across this great divide to the light beyond?"

Her feeble voice ended in a sob of fear. The son stroked her forehead to comfort her.

"Listen, mother, this man will tell you how to find the bridge."

Anching stroked her hand gently as he began to tell her that Jesus was the Bridge across the great chasm, and how that, by faith in Him alone she could find the way of salvation. As he explained the way to God through Jesus, she drank in every word.

"Oh, I can see the bridge," she exclaimed suddenly. "Just as you have been saying, there is a cross over the great chasm. I see some people walking over," she added excitedly. "Help me, I must get there before it is too late."

Anching repeated John 3:16. "This verse was not on the sheet your son found," he said. "Listen carefully, and believe in Jesus." He then quoted the old familiar verse: 'For God so loved the world that He gave His only begotten Son, that whosoever believes in Him should not perish, but have everlasting life.'

"Dear mother," he continued, "that word 'whosoever' means you. This is God's invitation to you to put your trust in Him. There is nothing more to do—no incense, no festivals to attend, no altar to sweep clean—just simply trust Jesus to open the way before you. Let Him take you by the hand and lead you across the chasm by way of the cross on which He died as your substitute."

The old woman gripped his hand tightly in hers, as her bony fingers pressed into his hand. "I can't see the way," she cried. "Oh, lead me to Him. I hear His voice calling me. Where is He?"

Anching prayed and asked that the Light of Jesus would flood her heart as she repented of her sins. As he prayed, her grip relaxed and, lifting her skinny arm toward heaven, she cried out with joy.

"Oh, Jesus, I am coming to You. Take me across the great divide and save my soul." She dropped her arm to her side as she continued. "The bridge! The bridge! It's right before me. Jesus has me by the hand. I am crossing the bridge," she murmured joyfully. "The light is getting brighter. Oh, thank you for coming in time."

The old woman slipped into a peaceful sleep, as her son continued to stroke her head.

"Thank you, Anching. You got here in time to help my mother. Come, let her sleep. You must tell the rest of the family this same story."

For the next hour Anching spoke to the assembled people and answered their questions. One by one they prayed to receive Jesus, until everyone in the room had prayed.

"We have waited so long to find out the whole story of Nicodemus and his search for God. Thank you for coming to tell us," the son spoke for all. "Now, come and have something to eat; and when you are finished, can you tell us more of the Bible's message?" he asked earnestly.

Gone was the weariness of body that Anching had felt. He ate with the family, and all the while they listened to more of the story of salvation. He talked long into the morning hours, as the thirsty people drank in every word. At four o'clock in the morning the people reluctantly returned to their homes, and Anching stretched himself on a bed and fell fast asleep. He was awakened by the sound of people rushing around, talking in loud voices.

"What's the matter?" he asked his host.

"Anching, my mother died peacefully a few minutes ago. She kept saying until her last breath, 'I've found the bridge. I'm crossing over and Jesus has me by the hand.' Anching, how can I ever thank you enough for coming to this remote place to lead my mother and all of us to Jesus!"

"Ah, my brother, there's no need to thank me. The only thing you all can do now for me is to spread this good news everywhere in this region."

"We will," assured the man. "Today, the whole village will assemble for my mother's funeral and I will tell them what happened to her last night. When I am finished, I want you to tell them more about The Way."

That afternoon, the whole village assembled in an open area near this man's home for the first Christian funeral they had ever witnessed. No firecrackers were exploded to frighten off evil spirits, no incense was burned, no loud wailing was heard. Instead, Anching taught them a song based on John 3:16:

Though dark the road on which I trod,
I come to You, dear Jesus,
And place my faith in You alone, the One who died for me.
I call upon Your Name for salvation from my sin.
I believe You died for me to find The Way to God.
I will follow You each day and give You my life,
As I journey on my way to heaven.

The song touched the hearts of the people as they sang it over and over again. The volume grew as they grasped the meaning of the words, until the little community rang with the joyful sound.

At the grave site Anching explained about the Resurrection and the hope every believer has. Many stood around the grave and prayed to receive Christ, as the story of the old woman was repeated again and again. They walked slowly back to the home and begged for more stories from the Bible.

But not everyone was happy about it. Although this community was isolated in the mountains and far from the larger centers where the Communists held sway, reports of this awakening reached the authorities. A small contingent of police was dispatched to the village to bring the leaders in for questioning.

"What is this we have heard about someone preaching about God in the village?" the officer in charge asked when they had all assembled before him.

"Anching stepped forward, and with a prayer in his heart, explained how he happened to come to the area. Taking his identity papers, the police officer examined them carefully, and then with a puzzled look on his face, asked him directly, "You are from Hong Kong. How is it that you are in this isolated village? And what is your destination? Your papers do not indicate where you are going. How do you explain that?"

"Sir, I am on my way to Puyang to visit my elderly parents.

"But this village is not on the way to Puyang," he insisted. "How is it that you are here?"

"Sir," he again replied, "I have no money to speak of, but I travel towards Puyang by whatever means I can. I arrived in this village by bicycle and will soon travel on toward Puyang when I am able to save enough money for the bus fare to the next town."

"That is very strange," replied the officer scratching his head. "I have never heard of anything like this before. Your papers are in order, as far as they go, but I must warn you that you are breaking the law by telling the people about God. Our Great Leader, Mao Zedong, has instructed us that there is no God, and certainly no Chinese should follow a Western god."

Anching chose his reply carefully.

"Sir," he began slowly. "I have been away from China for many years and I am unaware of many of the laws of my country. However, I want you to know that I am a loyal Chinese citizen who desires only to help the people find hope and peace in their hearts. I believe that is also what you desire for this area. Isn't that right?

"I am happy to report to you," he continued without waiting for an answer, "that since I arrived here there is more peace in the village than ever before. Fighting has ceased and neighbors are helping each other. It is already beginning to make your work easier. I hope you will allow us to return to the village to carry on this good work."

"But you must not hold meetings, nor spread any foreign, imperialistic propaganda; do you understand?" he asked sternly. "You are free to return," he continued, "only do nothing that brings you back into my office, or you will be punished severely." With that, he dismissed them all, after having taken down their names. Walking back to their mountain village, the people rejoiced that all had turned out well.

"We must be very careful," Anching admonished the people. "Although this is an isolated village, we must be careful not to cause the police to come again. Everyone must be careful to hide the sheets of Scripture that are being written down each day, and more must be done by word of mouth than in large gatherings. We must be careful how we share the gospel because, unfortunately, the government will send infiltrators into our midst as spies. However, as believers we must never stop spreading God's Word, even if it costs us our lives. I have returned to China to do just that. I know I may pay a very high price, but I will lean on God's Word at all times and trust Him to help me. I pray that each of you will do the same."

✓ The new believers responded with enthusiasm, promising to stand true under all circumstances. Day after day, more and more people came from the surrounding area to visit Anching and hear the story of the bridge to heaven.

One day, a man arrived from a village more than thirty miles away, seeking Anching, the young preacher.

"My wife is ready to deliver a child," he began, "but serious complications have developed. Her temperature is rising, and she is suffering intensely. It was reported in our village," he continued, "that you told the people here that your Jesus healed many people of all sorts of sicknesses and diseases. That person also told us that you said your Jesus is alive and He is all-powerful, and furthermore that He heals people today. Oh, please, come and pray for my wife and child," he pleaded.

Three men from the village volunteered to accompany Anching as he prepared to leave with the distraught man. Many other new believers, whom Anching was instructing every day, gathered to pray, and in simple, childlike faith, they asked God to heal the woman and bring glory to His Name throughout the region.

The small band made haste to leave since it would take eight or nine hours to reach the sick woman on foot. The pace was rapid, leaving little time for conversation or rest. Reaching the outskirts of the hamlet, they were greeted by a small party of villagers carrying lanterns.

"Hurry," they urged the husband, "your wife is dying."

Anching prayed that God would spare her life, at least long enough for him to speak with her. A small group had gathered at the home and had incense burning in an urn at the entrance to the home in anticipation of her approaching death.

Anching was ushered into the presence of the young mother writhing in pain on her bed. Kneeling beside her, he laid his hand upon her head and prayed for God to demonstrate His mighty power and deliver her baby. Curious villagers crowded in to watch, wondering what magic this man would use.

"Lord Jesus," he prayed, "Creator of heaven and earth, the only true and living God, hear my prayer and help this woman deliver her child. Prove Your mighty power to the people of this village and let your Name be magnified. And may many people, including this man and his wife, find their way to You and know Your wonderful salvation. I ask this in Your all-powerful Name. Amen."

As he was praying, the woman gradually ceased her tossing and lay quietly, while the husband stood nearby. A murmur arose among the people.

"She has been in pain for days. The writhing has been ceaseless for hours," they said to one another. "Look, she is resting. Who is this man, and who is this Jesus he speaks to?" they questioned among themselves.

"Is there a midwife here?" Anching asked the husband and the people.

"Yes, I am one," volunteered a woman standing by his side. She had been closely observing the unusual change that had taken place in the young woman and she was amazed. "What did you do to stop the pain?" she asked incredulously. "It has been going on for hours!"

"I will explain it all shortly, but now prepare some hot water and get ready to deliver the baby," he ordered. And addressing the people, he said, "The living God I serve is here tonight to demonstrate to all of you His great healing power. The mother will live and before long she will deliver a healthy child. Now, wait outside for the good news."

Reluctantly, the people vacated the room as the midwife continued to help the young mother. An hour later, a new life was ushered into the world. The news of the miraculous birth spread like wildfire through the hamlet, and people gathered to see the man who had worked such magic. For the next three days, Anching was tireless in explaining the way of salvation to all comers, until everyone had heard the gospel story.

Scores of people experienced the life-changing effects of the gospel. Throughout the mountain hamlet, singing could be heard ringing out over the hills from people who had never had anything to sing about before.

Satan, that old lying serpent, who had held the people of China in bondage for long, dark centuries was wounded by the victory of transformed lives, but he was not dead. He bided his time, uttering low, guttural sounds of dissatisfaction while he waited for the right moment to make a shattering comeback.

Chapter 11

ALL OF MY HEART

several weeks after Anching successfully crossed into China Meiling received her first letter from him, which told of God's miraculous intervention at the border.

"I am on my way north to find you once again," he exulted in the letter. "I have no idea when I will get there because I am practically penniless and committed to following the leading of the Lord all along the way. It seems God is leading me from house to house and village to village to preach His Word all the way back to you. At this point I do not have funds to make the journey directly to Taiping and, besides, it would be too dangerous to travel openly and run the risk of being apprehended by the police with travel documents that are questionable. So, please be patient. I am coming back."

Meiling was ecstatic. *Anching is coming*, as he had promised he would! *But when?* Her happiness settled into disappointment, knowing that the long-awaited meeting might be many weeks or months away. Still, the joy of knowing he was here in China and moving toward her, be it ever so slowly, caused her heart to leap with joy.

She opened her Bible to Psalm 31:14 and read: "I trust in You, O Lord; I say, You are my God. My times are in Your hands." She closed her eyes in prayer and praised God for His blessings in her life—and His promises, which had never failed. She would continue to wait.

Several days after the men returned from the mountain village two men in government uniforms rode into town on motorcycles, causing quite a stir among the villagers. Government officials rarely visited this remote town and, since the occupation of the country by the Communists, none had been in their town. Life had changed very little, but watching the men dismount, the shopkeeper that Anching was visiting turned to him and said, "I have a strange feeling they are looking for you. Go quickly to the field behind my shop and hide yourself under the shocks of wheat. I'll give you an all-clear signal as soon as possible."

Anching slipped away immediately, as the others busied themselves in the shop.

Hadn't Anching warned them that opposition from the government could develop at any time because of their newfound faith in Christ? many silently recalled. No one had long to ponder the question as the two men entered the store and demanded information.

"We are looking for a man by the name of Wen Anching, who was called into the police station for questioning a few weeks ago. Can you tell us where we can find him?"

The shopkeeper's heart skipped a beat as he intuitively sensed that this was going to be a serious confrontation. This new believer shot a silent prayer to God for help as he stalled for time. He wanted to be sure Anching was securely hidden. Though new in the faith, he was already fairly well grounded in the Word, and the Scripture Anching had discussed during the early morning prayer group flashed into his mind: You are awesome, O God, in Your sanctuary; the God of Israel gives power and strength to His people. (Psalm 68:35).

Lord, I claim your power and strength right now," he prayed silently.

"Why, yes, we know him, he replied honestly. "He's a fine young man we all like very much. He was here but he left, and I don't know where he is now."

Stepping closer to the shopkeeper, he pointed a finger in his face sternly. "I warn you not to trifle with the police. We were sent here to find this man. We have some questions to ask him. Anyone unwilling to cooperate with us, or hiding him, will be severely punished," he said, with a menacing tone in his voice.

"Sir," the shopkeeper responded, with a boldness that surprised even himself, "I have told you the truth. You may search my shop if you think I am hiding him here."

"Was he here this morning?" one of the men asked.

"Yes, he was," he replied, "but he left without telling us where he was going," he continued honestly. "He just returned from a trip to the hamlets to our north, but we don't know where he plans to go next."

As the police asked more questions they poked around the shop, looking under a table, behind some barrels containing rice, and in the room at the rear of the store. A young boy in the back of the store heard the questioning going on up front and, realizing that the intentions of the police were not good, slipped away unnoticed in order to warn the other believers. Meanwhile Anching had wormed his way under some shocks of wheat standing in the field behind the shop.

"Lord Jesus," he prayed, as he hid beneath the grain, *"I accepted the risk of imprisonment and even death when I returned to China to*

preach Your Word. Give me the strength and courage I need in this hour...and the wisdom to know what to do."

As he lay quietly he recalled the words of the German Pastor, Dietrich Bonhoeffer, whom Pastor Sung had quoted in one of his sermons some months ago. It flashed into his mind so clearly now, as if the pastor were by his side speaking at this very moment.

"When Christ calls a man, He calls him to die," Bonhoeffer had said. The first time the pastor repeated that sentence, it struck him powerfully. He recognized that the full cost of discipleship meant to take up his cross and deny himself. Now those words were recalled with new significance.

"Lord Jesus," he had prayed at the time, *"I surrender all to You. I give You my life, and I understand that I might die following You, but I withheld nothing from You; not even Meiling."*

From that moment onward he had started on a mission to reach his native land as a preacher of the gospel. The reality of that decision now struck him as he lay quietly under the shocks of wheat.

The word spread quickly among the loyal residents of the village that police officers were searching for Anching. After several hours of questioning people and receiving no leads as to where he was, the two officers finally mounted their motorcycles and sped off in a cloud of dust. Hearing the all-clear signal, Anching crawled out from under the wheat, brushed himself off, and made his way to the back room of the shop.

"Anching," the shopkeeper said urgently, "you must leave early in the morning. The police will be back. We will not be able to hide you. You must move on for your own safety."

"I know," he replied, "I must move on to protect you, also. I have been meditating on the cloud that guided the people of Israel through the wilderness. When it moved, the people moved. When it stood still, the people rested. I am depending on God to lead me in that same way. I believe the cloud has lifted, and I must follow where He leads me."

All evening people came to say goodbye and to thank him for sharing the gospel with them. As they left, they pressed a few coins into his hand and assured him they would be true to Jesus.

Very early the next morning, while it was still dark, Anching slipped out of the village on his way north. In his pocket was a letter of recommendation to friends in a town about forty-five miles away.

"They will receive you," assured the shopkeeper. "Share the good news with them, and let us build a network of Christian groups all across our nation so that all our people will hear about The Way."

Walking briskly along the road, Anching's heart was singing for joy. Not only was he obeying the Lord and following the cloud, but he was moving northward toward Meiling. As dawn was breaking in the eastern sky, a donkey cart overtook him. The driver stopped and invited him to ride with him. As he threw his pack on to the cart and climbed up next to the driver, he lifted his heart in prayer.

"Thank You, Jesus, for this ride. May it be a divine appointment for sharing the gospel with this man."

The overcast sky looked threatening on this sultry morning as the farmer urged his donkey on. "I am hoping to make it home before the storm hits," he said, as Anching settled in beside him. I still have about seven miles to go," he continued, eyeing the darkening sky. "How far are you traveling?" he asked.

Anching looked at him and smiled as he replied, "As far as possible. My destination is Puyang, and after that Taiping."

Surprised, the farmer looked at him and said, "Nowadays people can't travel that far because of restrictions. How did you get permission?" Anching explained the dual purpose of his journey—to visit his parents and find Meiling—as the two bounced along the rough road.

"You must have a lot of money in order to travel such a great distance," suggested the farmer after hearing the planned itinerary. "And besides, you will have to deal with the restrictions of the government all along the way."

"I am aware of that," Anching responded honestly. Then, turning toward the man he said, testing him, "We have been traveling along for more than an hour now. I have the feeling from our conversation that the policies of the new government are making life difficult for you."

Without responding to this statement the farmer commented, "And I have a feeling there is something different about you that makes you cautious of the government." He paused a moment for effect, and then asked pointedly , "Isn't that right?"

The exchange gave Anching confidence to proceed. Smiling, he answered. "I think we both understand each other. These are difficult days for everyone, and especially for those who believe in the living God."

"That's it!" replied the farmer. "I knew there was something different about you. You're like some people in my village who say the same thing. They believe in the living God, the Creator of the Universe. You're right. It is dangerous to hold such beliefs these days."

"I take it you do not believe," Anching ventured.

"Well, let's say I am impressed by these people, but I find it too dangerous to meet with them. You see, I hear they meet late at night to avoid detection. Some have been arrested, and some have been sentenced to prison. What would make anyone want to openly follow that kind of religion?"

"Jesus would make the difference," Anching replied, sensing that this man was honestly seeking the truth. "He gave His life to save me, and in turn I will give my life to serve Him."

"You mean even to imprisonment and suffering?"

"Yes, even to imprisonment and death!"

The farmer looked at him and responded slowly.

"That's the way they talk in my village, too. But why? Why would anyone risk suffering and death?"

For another hour the men conversed about why a believer was willing to give up everything in order to gain eternal life. The sky had darkened considerably, and now and then a streak of lightning flashed across the sky.

"It's a good thing we are almost home," said the farmer. "You must stay with us," he said congenially. "My wife will want to hear all these things that you have told me, and you will want to meet the believers in this town."

The next days were filled with lively conversations with the farmer and his wife, who both revealed a hunger for what Anching had to share. The believers of the village recognized his familiar voice as "the radio voice" that read Scripture over their shortwave radios. They crowded in to the small home to meet him personally. Displaying their handwritten Scriptures, the believers thanked him for each page they had copied. What impressed Anching the most was their devotion to Jesus, even though they had so little of His Word.

There was no Communist presence in these rural towns and so the people gathered freely. One Sunday, when several hundred people were deeply engrossed in listening to Anching's message, unexpectedly the cries of panic from people on the outer fringes of the crowd sent chills through the whole congregation. Police officers swinging batons broke into the crowd, shouting orders to remain seated. They pushed their way toward the makeshift platform and, grabbing Anching, demanded an explanation for this gathering.

"It is illegal in the People's Republic to hold gatherings like this that teach the imperialistic ideas of foreigners," shouted the officer as he pinned Anching's arms behind his back. The village elders, along with Anching, were rounded up and marched to the waiting van. Shocked and outraged, the people followed, shouting for the release of their friends. A cordon of policemen rushed toward the crowd, driving them back as they tossed teargas bombs into their midst. Bewildered, the crowd staggered backwards, shouting in pain from the teargas as the van drove quickly away. Grabbing some of the handwritten Scriptures from the unsuspecting people, the police threatened them with severe consequences if they did not stop holding such meetings.

Four village elders had been arrested. When they reached the city police station after a rough ride of over an hour-and-a-half, they were crammed into a small cell with hardly enough room for them to stretch out on the bare floor. A few hours after entering the cell, all four were taken to different rooms for interrogation. An hour later the interrogators changed and the same line of questioning began all over. Much of the interrogation centered on Anching, the one who was obviously leading the meeting.

"Who is he? Where did he come from? What did he say to the people? What was the response?" Hour after hour the questions were thrown at them like missiles, each interrogator seeking to find a vulnerable spot in the stories. Finally as dawn was breaking, they were returned to their cell, exhausted and hungry. The frightened men slumped to the floor and exchanged experiences, wondering what would happen next.

"Anching warned us to expect suffering if we entered the Jesus Way," said the farmer who had picked Anching up. "He explained to me several times that a believer in Jesus must take up his cross and deny himself, and follow Jesus. When I asked him what that meant, he said it meant that a person would love Jesus more than anything or anyone else in life, and that he would be willing even to die for Him."

"But it's so costly," replied one of the men. "Is it worth it to be humiliated and to suffer like this?"

The farmer noticed that the man was extremely weary and frightened. He replied carefully. "My friend, when I accepted Christ a few weeks ago, Anching taught me a verse of Scripture from the Bible in one of the books called Hebrews. It was written to encourage believers when they were in deep trouble. The verse says this: 'Never will I leave you; never will I forsake you. So we may say with confidence, The Lord is my helper; I will not be afraid. What can man do to me?" (Hebrews 13:6)

"Did Jesus say that?" asked the man, sitting up with interest and looking the farmer in the eye. "You mean when trouble like this comes to a believer Jesus is there to be his helper? Is that what it means?"

"That's what it means. And did you hear the end of that verse? It asks, 'What can man do to me?' As far as I know that means Jesus is our helper and He will not forsake us."

"This is all new to me," the man admitted, "but it makes sense. If Jesus is the Living God, then there is no one greater than He. And if Jesus is living in us, then He is here to help us. Is that right?" he asked again.

"That's what Anching taught me," the farmer replied. "Now brothers, I'm going to go to sleep on that promise. How about you?"

They all sighed in agreement and drifted off into much-needed sleep. Three days later they were freed to return to their homes. Wearily, they started walking back home, but their hearts were heavy. They could find out nothing about Anching.

Day after day the interrogations continued, sometimes for twelve or thirteen hours at a time. Anching's head was spinning from sleep deprivation, a favorite tactic used to elicit information from prisoners. The questioning centered on his unusual travel documents and the missing destination. "How could this be?" they asked him over and over again. He simply repeated the events in exactly the same way each time. "I have no explanation for this," he insisted. "The immigration officer returned my papers to me and sent me through the gate. That's all I can tell you," he reiterated. When asked the purpose of his trip and the length of time allowed for it, he simply referred to his papers—the documents issued by the Chinese government.

The interrogators were interested in the handwritten Scriptures they had confiscated. Anching was careful not to reveal that they were sections of the Bible, but he rejoiced as the officers read the words.

In his heart he prayed fervently. "Lord Jesus, make Your Word like arrows in their hearts...."

After almost three months of daily interrogations with little results, the police were unsure as to how to proceed. Since his travel documents were authentic, even though unusual, and his story was consistent and plausible, the chief finally decided to call the district office for advice. After considerable discussion it was decided to transfer him to the district prison.

Although he had not suffered any physical abuse during the three months he was imprisoned, he was weary in body and mind. He had been unable to communicate with his friends in the village, and he wondered how they had fared. *Were they still here in the prison? Had they stood true to Jesus after only a short time as believers?*

He would have to commit them to Jesus, who had promised to take care of His sheep at all times. Thinking about the delay in reaching Meiling was more difficult for him. *While I am preaching in town after town, I feel I am making progress toward the north,* he reasoned, *but being stuck here in this prison is such a waste of time!*

Alone, he struggled with his thoughts, and not having his Bible or anything to read, he lay on his hard bed in between the daily interrogations, quoting again and again the many chapters of the Bible he had committed to memory.

"We have been ordered to transport you to the district prison tomorrow," his interrogator announced one day. "Your case is most unusual, and so we have referred you to higher officials."

The announcement came like a bolt of lightning out of the blue. *Transferred to the district prison! More interrogations! More time in prison! More delays!* he cried in despair. *Oh, Lord,* he prayed, as he lay on his bed, *how long? How long will I be imprisoned? And clearly, I will not be able to return to the village. My possessions are few, but my Bible is there. What will I do without my Bible? Where will I find another one?*

Weary from the interrogations and feeling the great loss of his Bible, Anching tossed and turned for a long time until, finally, sleep overtook him. Some time during the night he awakened as a cold, chilly wind blew over him. There was something strange about the chill because it was still summer. The cell was stifling hot all the time. No cooling breeze had reached him in weeks. He sat up, searching for some answer to the mystery. He felt clammy all over and a deep sense of darkness surrounded him, even though the twenty-five watt bulb burned day and night. Then he heard a whisper in his ear.

"I warned you this would happen. It isn't worth it. You should have stayed in Hong Kong and married Sumei. She loved you and would have made you a wonderful wife. You have played the fool. You gave up freedom and a good wife for this ridiculous idea of preaching in China and finding Meiling. Ha! You are a fool! You're wasting your time. Better turn back while you can. Get your papers and go back to Hong Kong where it's safe."

As the chilly breeze blew against him, it suddenly seemed like a gale-force wind. He gripped the edge of his bed in order to keep from being blown over! In the corner of the cell he thought he saw two iridescent eyes glaring at him and heard a snarl like that of a wolf. Still gripping the bed, he wondered if all this was real or a dream.

Now the voice seemed to speak from the corner. *"Give up this foolish plan before it is too late. If you don't, you could spend the rest of your life in a cell like this. Then what? You have lost Sumei and you can't find Meiling. You'll rot in a miserable prison somewhere!"*

In those moments a great sense of aloneness swept over him, as the battering wind continued to buffet him. The voice was sinister and cruel, pushing him into a pit of despair. Suddenly a brilliant light filled the room, dispelling the darkness and the cold, eerie breeze. The dreadful eyes faded away in the warmth of the light and, in his heart, he heard the reassuring voice of Jesus comforting him.

"My son, I am here. Don't be afraid. You know I will never leave you alone, and I will deliver you. Satan has no authority over you. You are mine."

In a flash the words of Psalm 32 flooded his mind with comfort and assurance: "You are my hiding place; You will protect me from trouble and surround me with songs of deliverance. I will instruct you and teach you in the way you should go; I will counsel you and watch over you" (Psalm 32:6–8)

"Oh, my precious Jesus," Anching cried out to the Lord. *"Thank You for Your Presence and Your Word. I take my stand now upon Your Word and, with your help, I will not yield to Satan's temptations. I will follow You wherever You lead and give You my whole life. I will trust You, because I know Your Way is perfect.*

For the rest of the night he lay there, singing softly, as the peace of God flooded his soul. The words, "I will counsel you and watch over you," rang clear in his heart.

"I am all Yours, Lord," he spoke out loud. "You have all of me."

Chapter 12

. . . .

TRUST ME

More than six months after receiving Anching's letter informing her of his arrival in China, Meiling tried desperately to be patient. She had received no further word from him, and in such dangerous times that could mean trouble. She fortified herself with Scripture and carried on her work as discretely as possible. She continued her daily walks in various parts of town and always she was joined by someone in need of fellowship or encouragement.

The church is growing in spite of the harsh circumstances, she marveled, *as one by one seeking people come into a new relationship with Christ.*

Returning home one day from a long walk and conversations with several people, she was excited to see the notice that a parcel was waiting for her at the post office.

Who could be sending me a parcel? Not many people receive letters, let alone parcels, she thought, as she hurried to the post office. Picking it up, she quickly returned home with the tantalizing thought filling her mind, *Could this possibly be something from Anching? As* she opened the package, to her surprise she discovered it was a Bible!

How unusual to receive a Bible in the mail! It was forbidden. Everybody knew that.

Quickly opening the cover, she found a note tucked inside: "Woo Meiling," it read. "Several months ago Wen Anching arrived in our town...." Tears rushed to her eyes as she read those words.

Oh, praise the Lord, here's word from him, but why the Bible?

Hurriedly she returned to the letter. "For several months he lived in this remote area, traveling to many hamlets and villages to preach the gospel of our Lord Jesus Christ. Many unusual things happened in people's lives and many came into a relationship with Jesus Christ. But one Sunday about three months ago, the police from the city raided our meeting and arrested our village elders and Anching."

Her heart skipped a beat at the word arrest. *What tortures had he endured?* she wondered, recalling her own experiences. *And where is he now?*

Continuing on, she read: "The elders were released after three days of interrogation, but nothing has been heard from Anching until a few days ago. The head village elder had business in the city, and while there he visited the police station to inquire about Anching. All he could glean from them was that several weeks ago he was transferred to the district police station at the county seat. Anching often spoke about you, and since we do not expect him to return here, we are sending you his Bible. He prized it very highly. We would love to have kept it, but we know he must have it to continue his preaching."

Tenderly she flipped over the pages, noting the many verses he had underlined for emphasis. Her eye fell on the closing verses of Psalms 46, which Anching had boldly underlined. Her heart seemed to stop as she read the familiar words: "Be still and know that I am God; I will be exalted among the nations, I will be exalted in the earth. The Lord Almighty is with us; the God of Jacob is our fortress" (verse 10).

Oh, how precious that the Lord would send me this message at just this moment, she thought. *I don't know where Anching is, nor what his circumstances are, but here is God's promise that He is our Fortress and our Deliverer. Oh, thank You, Jesus, for I know You are in control of all things."*

Bewildered at the turn of events that had come upon him, Anching just stood in the middle of the road and watched the police van disappear in a cloud of dust. Not knowing what to make of his strange travel documents, and not wanting to get involved in this unusual case, the district police chief had decided to just transport him to the next county and drop him off in another jurisdiction. It suddenly dawned on Anching that he had been miraculously delivered from prison—just as Peter had been! This was not a dream! He was a free man!

But, now what? he thought. *I don't have any money, and I own only what's on my back!* "Lord," he prayed, "it looks like You're going to have to work another miracle."

The road led north so he started walking along, singing a song of praise. It was late afternoon when he approached a small cluster of buildings where several children were playing. An elderly woman sat in the doorway, preparing vegetables for the evening meal. As he approached she looked up from her work with a surprised look on her face.

"Hello, grandmother," Anching called as he approached. "My name is Wen Anching. I'm on my way to the big city of Puyang up north. May I rest here awhile?" he asked with a pleasant smile. The children gathered around, looking the stranger over from head to foot. It wasn't every day that a visitor came to their small hamlet.

"Welcome," she called, with a friendly wave of her hand. "Come, and sit down. I'll get you some tea," she said. Then, pausing and looking at him directly, she asked, "How is it that a young man like you is walking along this road? Most young men are in the army and the older ones are working at the commune."

"I know, grandmother," he replied. "I am on a long journey to visit my elderly parents who live in Puyang. I have not seen them in more than twenty years. Fortunately, I was given permission to return to see them."

Sitting in the shade of the house sipping the hot tea, he had the strong feeling that God had guided him to this place for a special purpose. He listened to the woman recite the woes the family had been encountering in recent years. Perhaps because this isolated area had little contact with government authorities people still trusted one another and were freer to talk about conditions. She seemed to hold nothing back.

"The government authorities have demanded the consolidation of all the farms into one large commune," she said. "We are no longer free to plant what we want, and there are always quotas to be reached. Everything we raised is controlled by the government, and in return, we're issued a mere pittance to live on.

"Life has become very hard and difficult," she continued, carrying on with her litany of complaints. "The old China was never like this," she moaned. "All this used to be our family's farm, but now it has been taken over by the commune. We are allowed only that little piece of land for our own use," she whimpered pointing with a bony finger to the small plot of land they called their own. "It is a crime to have your land stolen from you," she added vehemently.

"I understand, grandmother," Anching responded sympathetically, "but you ought not to be criticizing the government to a stranger. Spoken to the wrong person, it could cause you and your family much grief," he admonished.

"Young man," she said, with a knowing nod of her head. "I know that, but I have lived a long time, and I know a good man when I see one, and you're one who can be trusted," she said with a toothless smile.

"Thank you, grandmother. I try to live my life in such a way that I will always please my God," he replied, with a little less caution after the compliment she had given.

"*Ah ha!*" she said, with another nod of her head. "I knew you must be a religious man. There is something about you that attracts me. Tell me, what god do you worship?"

"Grandmother," he answered with his engaging smile, "I worship the True and Living God, the Creator of the World, and the Savior of all Mankind!"

"I never heard of Him," she answered honestly. "Tell me, does He answer your prayers?"

"Indeed He does. When I pray to the Living God, He is always there to listen and to help me."

"Really? You mean your God actually hears you and answers you? Mine doesn't. I pray all the time, but I never get answers. Take our pig, for example. It has been very sick for several days. We have tried everything we know to help it get better. If it dies, it will be a great financial loss to our family. For several days now I have been burning incense and asking my god to make the pig well, but there is no answer. In fact, the pig is worse now than ever, and unless something happens, it will die."

Having said that, her face suddenly lit up with a big smile as if someone had turned on a light.

"Young man, if your God is so strong and actually hears your prayers, will you pray that our pig gets better? If it does, I will know that your God is greater than mine."

Anching suddenly remembered his thoughts of a few hours ago when he was dumped off at the border that God would have to work a miracle to help him out of his situation.

Lord Jesus, he prayed, *You asked me to trust You in every circumstance, and I do. Now here's a test that will open up the heart of this old woman, and perhaps many others. Help me and answer my prayer for this sick pig.*

Before he had opportunity to answer the woman, the children began shouting.

"Here they come, grandmother."

She looked up to see the men and women of the family returning from the field. As they trooped into the courtyard, they stopped and looked at Anching sitting there.

"And who is this?" asked the father, as he eyed Anching suspiciously. For the next few minutes the grandmother explained all she knew about Anching. Judging from the expressions on their faces the father and the others seemed pleased.

"So, you are traveling through to Puyang?" asked the father. "Grandmother tells us you are a good man and a religious one at that. She has a keen sense of judging character and we all trust her judgment. You have passed the test, and we welcome you to our humble home. But what is this she has been telling us about your God answering your prayers?"

"Thank you, sir, for your kind hospitality. Grandmother has been asking me many questions, and I am glad she considers me a good man. As to my God, yes, He does answer my prayers. He is alive, the Living and True God, the Creator of the Universe, and Savior of all Mankind!"

"Grandmother has made a proposal. She wants you to pray for our sick pig, and if the pig gets better she says she wants to worship your God. We are in agreement. To lose our pig is to lose everything we have saved for a whole year. Yes, if your God heals the pig, we will worship your God."

"Then, let us go to the pen and I will lead us all in prayer to the Living God," answered Anching with anticipation.

The small group trooped out to the pigpen. There lay the sow with bloated stomach, groaning in distress and looking as if she would die at any moment. Everyone gathered around, staring at Anching and wondering what was going to happen. He took a few minutes to explain about the Living God and how much He loved the people of the world. He also explained the power and effect of prayer and why God delights in helping His children.

At last he squatted down beside the sow, laid his hands on her, and began to pray a simple prayer for the healing of the pig and the salvation of the family. Everyone listened attentively, while watching expectantly for something to happen. Anching concluded his prayer and, standing, spoke to the people in the circle.

"Now, let's wait and see what my God will do for you. I believe He will answer my prayer and heal your sow. I hope you will be convinced that He is the true and living God, and that you will worship Him alone."

"You must eat the evening meal with us," said the father, "and stay with us tonight. Then in the morning we will see if your God has answered your prayers and healed our pig."

Everyone rose at daybreak, ready for another long day of work. Suddenly the sound of someone shouting shattered the quietness of the morning.

"Everyone come quickly!" cried one of the younger boys who tended the pig. "Our pig is standing! It is better. Hurry, come quickly." Every member of the family rushed to take a look at the pig. Even the old grandmother hobbled out as fast as she could to see it. To the amazement of all, there stood the pig, wide-eyed and tail wiggling as it looked around expectantly for food.

"Grandmother, look," they shouted. "Look! Anching's God healed our pig!"

Anching stood in the background enjoying the excitement and praising God for what He had done.

"Anching, bless you, young man," exclaimed grandmother. "Your God answered your prayer. He must be the living and true God. Oh, please, do not leave us today. You must tell us more about how to worship Him."

The father bowed politely to Anching as he said, "Grandmother is right. You must not leave us today. We want to know who this God is. We will hurry home from work tonight, and then you will tell us everything we need to know."

"That will be a very special privilege," Anching responded with a smile. "Tonight I will tell you all about the God who answers prayer."

As the whole family gathered under a large tree in the cool of the evening, there was a buzz of voices every time the pig squealed. The father of the clan exclaimed excitedly, saying over and over again, "Anching, you saved us from financial disaster! How can we ever thank you enough?"

Grandmother spoke up, also. "But more important than that is the fact that Anching has a God who answers prayer. I'm an old woman, and soon I will pass into the next life. I want to hear how to worship 'the God who answers prayer.'"

For two hours Anching explained the way of salvation as simply as he could, until all their questions were answered. Finally the father spoke for the whole family.

"Anching I am ready to pray and ask forgiveness for my sins. You have answered all our questions, and we have seen the power of your God demonstrated in our own home. Now we want to believe."

One after another all in the circle spoke, stating their desire to believe. That evening, twelve people prayed to receive Christ. Anching taught them a song based on Matthew 6:25–34 that was popular among believers elsewhere in China:

Our Heavenly Father is great in mercy.
He feeds and clothes us every day.
We will worship and humbly learn from Him,
`For our Lord clothes the grass of the field.

Do not worry what we shall eat today,
Or what we shall drink tomorrow.
Surely our Heavenly Father will sustain us.

Look at the little sparrows, flying to and fro,
Look at the lilies in the field; they do not labor or spin,
Yet the Lord dresses them in all their splendor.
Are we not much more valuable than these?

Brother, change your heart and follow Christ,
For this world is not your home.

—Brother Yun, from *The Heavenly Man*

Bubbling over with joy, the family members remarked after each time they sang the song: "We have never sung a song like this. Our old religion had nothing in it to make us sing. We never knew we could be saved and have eternal life. Now, thanks to you, Anching, we have accepted Jesus, and we will walk in the Way of Life.

"Tomorrow night we will invite our neighbors to hear your message," stated the father emphatically. "You don't need to leave us yet, do you?" he asked in a pleading voice. "There is so much we want to learn. You must stay with us and teach us."

"Good," responded Anching enthusiastically, and tonight we will begin to write down some passages of Scripture that I will recite for you. No one can continue in the Christian life without God's Word. You will memorize these pages so that God's Word will be stored in your heart for the future. Unfortunately, the Communist government officials do not want us to own any part of the Bible. You must guard your pages as the most precious possession you have, and follow all the instructions they teach you."

"What does the Bible look like?" asked a young girl in the circle. "Where is yours?" she persisted.

"One of the saddest things happened to me in the last town that I ministered in. I was imprisoned for several months for leading a meeting in the village. When I was arrested, my Bible was left behind. The only one I have now is in my heart and mind. I have memorized large portions of it and will recite it beginning tonight so that we can all write it down and treasure it."

"Can't we get started now?" another young girl asked. "Or, at least, can you tell us more stories of Jesus. I liked that one about Him feeding the five thousand people."

"Tonight we will start writing down some passages of Scripture and, then tomorrow we will have time for more stories," Anching replied with a smile as the children hugged him warmly.

Two weeks passed very quickly as Anching continued to spread the Word through the area and people responded to the message. Many received Christ as their Lord and Savior and some were healed. The songs Anching taught them touched many hearts.

"We will never forget you, Anching," the people said, as they walked with him to the next town, about five miles away, where he could get a bus north. One of the men handed him a bus ticket and pressed some money into his hand.

"Come back as soon as you can," he said. "You are always welcome. We want to learn more of The Way to heaven."

"Stay in touch with the believers in the other towns where I have been and we will build a network of churches across our land," Anching replied as he waved goodbye to his new friends before boarding the bus.

As he bounced along the rough road, Anching prayed to God for guidance. *The cloud has lifted*, he thought, as he watched the countryside passing by, and looked forward to his next resting place. *I wonder what the next stop will be like.* Again the words of Psalm 32 flashed into his mind: "I will instruct you and teach you in the way you should go. I will counsel you and watch over you" (Psalm 32:8).

Arriving at his destination he stood looking around, wondering what God had in store for him this time. "I am trusting You, Lord Jesus, to guide my steps and lead me to the place where I can serve You." As he stood there, he heard a soft whisper.

"Pingan" (peace), a man whispered in his ear, "and may God bless you. You are the man I saw in my dream. I was sent to bring you to my home. Follow me," he instructed softly, as he walked on ahead.

"I sent him," God's voice sounded in Anching's heart. *"Go with him and don't be afraid."* Excited that God was fulfilling His promise, Anching took off after the man.

"I am a pastor," the man said, as they reached an isolated stretch of road. "Last night, God spoke to me in a dream and instructed me to come to the station to meet a man on whom the Spirit of the Lord is resting. *'He is a choice servant of Mine,'* the Lord said to me in my dream. *'Take him to your home, for he will bless the believers.'* So, who are you and what has God been doing in your life?"

Anching shared his experiences as the pastor listened.

"My heart is warmed to hear you talk," he said at last. "I believe God has sent you to us to help us spread His Word. It will not be easy, though. I have been called in several times for questioning. The last time they kept me several days and beat me severely, but I rejoice that when one serves the Lord, he does not just suffer for Jesus, he suffers with Jesus. My days in prison were the most glorious days I have lived because I was experiencing the Presence of Jesus in a most unusual way."

"I have had the same experience," Anching replied. "It seems that in times of deepest trouble and suffering, Jesus is there to lift me up and carry me through. I can honestly say that my cell has been a beautiful sanctuary at times…because Jesus shared it with me."

The days flew by quickly as the two men bonded together in ministry.

"Oh, Pastor Tan," commented Anching one day, "my heart yearns for the new believers in the towns I have passed through. They have no Bibles to nourish and instruct them in God's ways, and they have no pastors to guide them. How I wish there was a way to duplicate sections of the Bible for the people. Without it, they will wilt and die."

"I know," replied the pastor sorrowfully, "the only Bible my congregation has is the one I own. There are several hundred people scattered throughout this region who believe in Jesus, but because of government restrictions we have never all been together for a meeting. I meet with them secretly in small groups or individually and share God's Word. They beg me for a Bible, but I have none to give them."

"If only we had a way to print sections of the Bible," Anching mused. "There must be a way…."

"Maybe there is," said the pastor as a new thought struck him. "Before the Communists took over in our city," he spoke up with growing excitement, "there was a missionary who lived here. He had some kind of a machine that he used to print lessons for the children."

"He did?" Anching jumped to his feet in his excitement. "By any chance, is it still around somewhere? I think it is a mimeograph machine. I used to operate one for the hospital in Hong Kong."

"I don't know, but there is an old man living here who used to work for the missionary. Let's go and ask him about it."

"It would be a miracle if it was still around," Anching said, as his smile faded into a frown, but let's go and find out."

An hour later they had found the old man, who was seated outside his little home. As he listened to the pastor a smile began to creep across his face.

"Pastor, when the missionary had to leave, he asked me to take care of his mimeograph," he began.

Anching quickly interrupted. "Do you know where it is?

"Yes," he replied. "My old friend Li, the owner of the rice shop, has it stored away in a secret place, waiting for the day the missionary returns."

"Really?" exclaimed the pastor. "We hold meetings in his home sometimes. He is a true believer. Anching, this is the miracle you were speaking about!"

Arriving at Brother Li's shop, the old pastor began to question him.

"Brother Li, you know that package the missionary asked you to store for him several years ago? It was a machine that he used to print lessons for the children. Do you still have it around somewhere?"

"It is right where I stored it," he replied softly, "and no one but you knows I have it. I have never even told my wife about it. The police would be very angry with us if they knew we were storing something for the foreigners."

"You're right," replied the pastor. "It must not be known beyond this circle."

"I have it stored in a secret place and no one could ever find it," he said with a twinkle in his eyes. Then, looking at Anching, whom he had never met, he paused and looked questioningly at the pastor.

"Anching is a trusted believer," replied the pastor. "In fact, it was his idea to find some way to duplicate portions of the Bible for the believers. He told me he used to use a similar machine in Hong Kong."

"I trust your judgment, pastor," replied Brother Li, "but as you know, one cannot be too careful these days. I mean no offense to you, Anching, but I would feel better telling only Pastor Tan where it is hidden."

"No problem," responded Anching cheerfully. "I understand perfectly."

As the two men returned from a room behind the shop, the pastor spoke solemnly.

"Let's go. We have lots to think about." After they had said farewell to the old man, Pastor Tan turned to Anching and said, "I can see already that God has sent you here for a very special purpose. Brother Li has the mimeograph machine stored in a very safe, secret location. I believe that it is important that as few people as possible know anything about it or we may lose a great opportunity to spread God's Word."

"That's wonderful, Pastor Tan. Now when can I see the machine and determine if it is still in workable condition?"

"I knew you would ask that," he said with a smile. "Tonight, after Mr. Li closes his shop."

Some time after 10 P.M. Pastor Tan and Anching made their way stealthily to Mr. Li's shop.

"We must be very careful not to be noticed," the pastor said, as he guided Anching through the shadows to the shop's back door.

"Yes, I agree," Anching whispered, "because if the machine is workable, we will be able to print and circulate pages of Scripture to all of the believers.

"You're right, Anching. The believers need Scripture to mature in Christ. I have been praying that after all these years the machine will still be usable."

Slipping in the back door, Mr. Li greeted them warmly. He too understood the significance of using the mimeograph machine to print God's Word. Turning to Anching he spoke gravely, "Young man, I am going to reveal something to you that most members of my family know nothing about. I am doing this for the sake of the gospel, but in doing so, I am placing myself and my family at great risk. I trust you because you are Pastor Tan's friend and because the Lord has given me peace in my heart about you."

"Mr. Li," Anching replied solemnly, "you will never be disappointed in me. I returned to China at great personal risk because my goal is to reach as many people with the gospel as possible. I will die rather than reveal your secret to anyone."

"Good. Then let me show you an old cave behind my shop wall. This building is more than one hundred years old. It was built against the entrance to a mountain cave. Only a few family members living today know anything about it, and they are all believers." He pointed to the wall and challenged his listeners. "Gentlemen, can you find the entrance to the cave from where you are standing?" he asked with a satisfied smile.

Both men looked carefully at the shelves lining the wall but saw nothing out of the ordinary.

"You will have to show us the secret entrance," Pastor Tan remarked finally.

Mr. Li smiled as he motioned toward a small box attached to the wall.

"I use that as a seat sometimes," he said, "when I do my accounts. Behind that is the entrance to the cave!"

Both men edged forward in order to see more clearly in the dim light. Taking hold of the box seat, he tugged on it gently. Both men watched in awe as it began to move away from the wall. In a few seconds, Mr. Li pulled the box seat aside, revealing a dark hole about two-and-a-half feet square.

"There it is," he said with a chuckle. "I store my valuables in there for safe keeping."

Taking a small lantern he got down on all fours and prepared to crawl into the hole.

"Follow me. Don't be afraid, pastor," he said, patting him on the shoulder. "This small entrance opens into a large room after just a few feet. That's where the mimeograph machine is stored—and it's still in its original wrapping."

Anching's heart raced with excitement. *Could it be that God had prepared for this day so many years ago? And would the machine still be useable? What about stencil supplies for this old machine? I guess I'll just have to wait and see what condition the machine is in*, he thought, as he waited his turn to crawl in.

By the time Anching reached the end of the small tunnel, Mr. Li was standing inside the cave, holding up the lantern to give better light. Both men gasped as they saw the size of the cave. It was roughly fifteen feet square and about nine feet high! At some time in the distant past, someone had hollowed out this place, probably as a secret vault to store valuables.

"Here is the machine our old friend brought to me after the missionary left back in 1949. It has never been opened."

Anching knelt down on the floor and began to untie the cord that bound it. Pulling back the wrapping, which was stained in some places from the oily ink of the drum, the three men looked at the old machine. With fingers tingling with excitement, Anching took hold of the drum handle and cranked it slowly. It moved easily.

"Praise the Lord!" he exclaimed. "I think I can clean this up and make it work!"

"There's something else under the machine," Pastor Tan said as he pulled the wrapping away.

"Stencils!" Anching guessed as he slid the flat box out from under the machine. "If there are unused stencils in here, we are in business!" he exclaimed with mounting excitement. Lifting the cover off the box, he gently pulled out a stack of stencils, all beautifully preserved. In addition, there were half-a-dozen stylus pens needed for writing.

"This is a miracle," he breathed. "With these stencils I can write out Scripture portions and get them printed. Oh, Pastor Tan, do you realize what this discovery means? Your people will be able to hold the Word of God in their hands."

"More than that, Anching," exclaimed the pastor, "most of these believers have never owned a Bible—not even a page of one. They will hold the Word of God in their hands for the first time in their lives!"

"Pastor, let's give thanks to God right now," Anching said, as he pulled the box of stencils close to his heart. "Let's also pray that no one will discover our secret and that God will open a door for the Word to spread rapidly."

The three men bowed in prayer with grateful hearts, knowing that long before the present scourge had swept over the land, God had prepared for this moment.

When they were finished they rose from their knees as Anching addressed the two men about his vision and plan to prepare the Scripture pages. "I have a plan I believe God is giving me. Before your shop opens each day, I will come and crawl in here. You will close up the entrance until after you close your shop for the day. I will use that time to prepare the machine, write the stencils, and do the printing," he said as the two men listened attentively.

"But you cannot stay in here for seventeen to eighteen hours a day!" exclaimed Pastor Tan with concern. "That would be like being in jail."

"Pastor," Anching laughed, "I was confined to a cell much smaller than this for more than three months in the last town I preached in. I am used to it and, besides, I will be very busy. There's no time to lose. What do you think of my plan?"

"It will be very uncomfortable for you, but it will work," Mr. Li replied. "My wife will prepare food and water for the day. It is the only way, Pastor Tan, if we want God's Word to be printed."

The pastor nodded his head slowly, in amazement at Anching's enthusiasm.

"You are a remarkable man," he said, grasping his hand. "God sent you to us for just this very hour. Oh, praise the Lord, and may His Word spread rapidly."

"Amen," the two men repeated together.

"Then I will be here before daybreak tomorrow," Anching declared. I will need some old rags and some turpentine to clean the machine, a small box to be used as a table, and a stool." Pausing a moment, he laughed as he added, "And some food and water, too; otherwise it will be too much like my prison cell," he chuckled.

"Done," exclaimed Mr. Li with a smile as they prepared to exit the cave.

"But, remember, our lives depend on secrecy," Pastor Tan added solemnly. "No one must know where you are or what you are doing. Lord, help us and give us the victory over Satan."

"We will stand on the Word in Philippians," Anching added. "Remember, it says, 'I can do everything through Him who gives the strength'" (Philippians 4:13).

Chapter 13

THE MIRACLE

Meiling could hardly contain her excitement as she opened a letter from Anching. Her heart skipped a beat as she read that he was in Hunan Province and anxiously waiting for God to open the door for him to return to the adjoining Province of Hubei, where Puyang was located.

"Sometimes God moves so slowly," he wrote, "but He never fails to move. I am involved in a most exciting work right now that I cannot share here, and just when it will be finished, I have no idea. I only know that, like the people of Israel, I move when the cloud lifts and I stop when the cloud stops. I wait patiently for the Lord to open the door to see you again, but we must be prepared for more delays, as Satan is opposing everything I am doing. Thank God, I am more than a conqueror through our Lord Jesus Christ. For a man who has no money and improper travel papers, I am making remarkable progress. It is the Lord working His miracles every day."

Meiling read Anching's letter over and over again as she praised the Lord for the miracles He was doing for him.

Some day, she thought, *we will be able to tell each other about the many miracles God has wrought in bringing us back together. For now I will rest in the Lord and wait patiently for the answer to my prayer.*

The twenty-year sentence of Pastor Yang, the courageous pastor from Puyang who had been working in the stone quarry since 1952, was drawing to a close. During those years, hundreds of men had quietly embraced Christ because of his godly example and his steadfast testimony. Of those who had survived the rigors of the quarry, many went on to become the backbone of the growing church that could not be overcome.

The vision God gave to Pastor Yang years before of starting a Bible training school upon his release was burning in his heart with greater fervor than ever before.

"*Lord Jesus,*" he prayed one day, "*I believe that I will survive this horrible place and live to fulfill the vision You have given me. Strengthen me for the remaining years of my life so that I may have a part in reaching China through the young people you send to me. And may these men and women catch the vision of taking the gospel even beyond the borders of our country.*

"*Lord, help me to prepare them to take the gospel westward through all the lands between China and Jerusalem. The years of hardship and persecution here in this prison camp have prepared me to teach them the cost of following You. And, Lord, may the whole world know that it is not enough to follow You in pleasant places. May the world know that the Church in China is prepared to take the gospel to the ends of the earth—and even through the most painful experiences of persecution and death—so that millions will be added to Your Kingdom!*"

With his heart bursting with the vision of a growing, vibrant church in China despite the years when all churches were closed,

Bibles banned, and most pastors imprisoned, he fervently prayed for courage and strength. Yes, he would have much to do when he was released.

The little cave behind the rice shop had more to do with turning lives around than almost any other activity of the underground church. Day after day Anching labored at meticulously writing down the Scriptures in order to encourage and build up the ever-expanding number of believers. In consultation with Pastor Tan it was decided that the first page of Scripture he gave the people should include passages from the Psalms.

"The believers need the hope and consolation of the Psalms," Pastor Tan suggested. "Give them Psalm 23, 27, and 34 to start with."

With these instructions, Anching had carefully transcribed those Psalms onto the fragile stencils. His one concern was whether or not the twenty-year-old stencils would be strong enough to print hundreds of pages for the believers. Crawling out of the cave on the tenth day of work, he beamed with excitement as he handed the first page of Scripture to the pastor.

With trembling hands, the pastor took the page and began to read the beautifully written characters: "The Lord is my shepherd. I shall not want" (Psalm 23:1). Tears sprang to his eyes as he read through the chapter. Gripping Anching in a strong embrace, he wept as he spoke from his heart.

"Today the Church has come alive! Soon hundreds of God's people will hold these precious portions of His Word in their hands and read them for themselves. Anching, you have opened the door for the people of this region to hear God speak to them through His Word. Here, Brother Li, touch it, kiss it, and read it yourself!"

It was a sacred moment the three men never forgot. Twenty-three years after the takeover by the Communists, one printed page of God's Word was ready for circulation.

Several months had passed since the Word began to circulate among the believers. Anching worked tirelessly to prepare other pages of Scripture, and each was received with tears and prayers of praise and thanksgiving. Pastor Tan instructed the people on how to preserve their sheets from detection by the authorities and, above all else, how never to divulge where they'd come from. As some twenty people gathered secretly one night, concern was expressed that the growing number of believers increased the danger of arrest. The danger came from those who only professed to be believers, but in actuality were spies of the government determined to ferret out and destroy all believers.

Their worst fears were realized one night as they were quietly praying. Shouting police officers raided the home where Pastor Tan was leading the gathering. Frantically the people tried to hide the sheets of Scripture, but it was too late. Rounded up and carted off to the police station with five incriminating sheets of Scripture that had turned up as police officers had ransacked the home, the believers came under merciless beatings and threats.

No one revealed their secret. Pastor Tan and Anching were isolated from the others and each of them, in turn, endured the most severe beating either had ever experienced. When one police officer tired of beating them, another stepped in to continue the torture.

"We have examined the printed material we seized at the time of the illegal meeting, and we have discovered that these sheets are identical," stated one interrogator. "Where did you get them from? Who is printing them and where are they being printed?"

After several hours of interrogation and beatings, Pastor Tan was brought back to his cell and dumped on the floor, as Anching was hauled out for his turn. Though wounded and bleeding, they gave nothing away.

"Did you get these from a foreigner who sneaked into our country?" they screamed. "These must have come from outside of China," they argued. Every form of coercion was applied without success. The second day, police raided the homes of the people in custody, tearing everything apart in an effort to locate the source of the sheets. In the course of the interrogation and beatings of the other believers, one man broke under the intensity of the beating. He confessed that Anching had often instructed them from the sheets that came from the Bible.

With his back bruised and bleeding from several days of beatings, Anching was dragged into the torture room once again.

"We know you are a newcomer to our town," began the interrogator. "You must be responsible for the sheets of forbidden Scripture that we discovered," shouted the officer, with venom in his voice.

"I will beat you until you tell us the truth," he snarled. To emphasize his point he had a rookie police officer strike him five times with a bamboo pole.

"More is coming unless you tell me the whole story," he threatened. Unsuccessful in illiciting any answer from him, he ordered him handcuffed to a pole with his hands above his head. Taking the bamboo pole from the officer, he swung it viciously at Anching's legs. It struck his shins with a sickening thud that caved in his legs, knocking him off his feet, only to have his fall suddenly halted as his full body weight tore at his wrists, which were handcuffed to the pole. Excruciating pain coursed through every muscle of his body. Struggling to his feet again, a second blow crashed against his body, sending him into a spasm of pain.

Gritting his teeth to keep from screaming, he answered the repeated interrogator's question, "Where did these sheets come from?" by gasping out the words, "From the living God in heaven."

Incensed, the policeman whacked him repeatedly, until he just hung there groaning with intense pain.

"Take him down and return him to his cell," the officer ordered. Almost unconscious and unable to walk, Anching was dragged down the hallway to his cell and dropped with a terrible thud on the cold cement floor. With great effort Pastor Tan struggled to rise from his cot to help him.

"Oh, my poor brother, what have these monsters done to you?" Only with intense difficulty was he able to drag Anching to his cot and get him off the floor. Exhausted himself, he tried to comfort him, but all he could do was pray for his unconscious brother. He sank down on his cot and wept until drained of all emotion, he finally lapsed into a fitful sleep, where he found some relief at last.

During the painful days that followed, both men encouraged each other with Scripture and prayer. Since Anching had committed whole books of the Bible to memory, he taught them to this country pastor until he, too, was repeating long sections of the Word. Although their bones ached from the beatings and both found it difficult to stand or walk, they both rejoiced and sang songs because they had been counted worthy to suffer with Jesus.

A few days later Pastor Tan was brought back to the cell after several hours in the interrogating room. As soon as the door was closed and they were alone, he sat down on Anching's bunk and said quietly, "Anching, I have been sentenced to three years of re-education with hard labor. I will be leaving tomorrow morning."

"Three years in prison?" Anching exclaimed with horror. "It's all my fault. It's because I printed those pages of Scripture that you must suffer."

"No, no, no, my dear brother! It's not your fault at all. It's because I have chosen to follow Jesus and spread His Word. I knew full well the cost of spreading His Word. It's the price we all must pay in order to be true to Jesus. Now I can rejoice that while I am gone the believers will have some portions of the Bible to help and comfort them, and even if you and I cannot be there, someone else will use the cave to print God's Word."

"Brother Li begged me to teach him how to use the mimeograph to do just that. He told me that if I was arrested or needed to leave, someone needed to be ready to step in and take my place. I trained him just last week."

Pastor Tan sat down by his side and together they repeated Scripture to bolster their faith. Let's sing that song you taught us from Acts—the one written by a pastor in prison. Their spirits were lifted as they sang.

And now, compelled by the Spirit, I am going to Jerusalem,
Not knowing what will happen to me there.
I only know that in every city the Holy Spirit warns me,
That prisons and hardships are facing me.

However, I consider my life worth nothing to me,
If only I may finish the race,
And complete the task the Lord Jesus gave me:
To testify to the gospel of God's grace.

—Brother Yun, from *The Heavely Man*

The next morning the two men prayed together and held each other in a close embrace.

"Be faithful unto death," Anching said to his friend.

Nodding in agreement, Pastor Tan answered him. "I will. And we shall inherit a crown of life."

The door of the cell opened, and Pastor Tan was led out. As it clanged shut again, Anching strained to hear the fading footsteps of his friend being led away to a slave-labor camp.

And what will my sentence be? he wondered. *Three years? Or ten? Pastor Yang was given twenty years!* A lump formed in his throat. *It was more than twenty-three years ago now that I promised Meiling I would find her if it took the rest of my life, and here I am only one province away! So close, but a prisoner!*

"Lord," he prayed, *"what lesson do You want me to learn this time?"*

The words in Matthew's Gospel came to mind. "Anyone who loves his father or mother more than me is not worthy of me; anyone who loves his son or daughter more than me is not worthy of me; and anyone who does not take up his cross and follow me is not worthy of me. Whoever finds his life will lose it, and whoever loses his life for my sake will find it" (Matthew 10:37–39).

As he pondered the implications of these words, a new song formed in his mind and he began to sing:

> The days of our pilgrimage may be dreary and long,
> And the road filled with suffering and pain,
> But Jesus calls us to follow wherever He leads,
> And love Him with all our hearts.
> Sometimes I feel discouraged because the way is so long,
> But then Jesus speaks in the darkness, "Fear not, I am
> with you."
>
> So I'll love Him and serve Him with all of my heart,
> All of my soul, and all of my mind.
> I'll love You, Lord Jesus, all of my days,
> And rest in Your wonderful care,
> Until at last I am safely home in the place You're
> preparing for me.

As these words poured forth from his yielded, contrite heart, his dark, miserable cell was transformed into a sanctuary where the glory of God's Presence permeated every corner. Scripture kept flooding his mind as the hours passed until dawn. From a heart bursting with the joy of the Lord, he called out loudly: "I will bless the Lord at all times; his praise shall continually be in my mouth" (Psalm 34:1 KJV).

A guard opened a peephole and looked in on this amazing scene—a prisoner severely beaten, alone in his dark cell, singing and speaking joyfully to himself!

These Christians are the strangest people I have ever met, he thought to himself as he closed the slot and moved on.

Several days passed without Anching's having any contact with another human being, except at meal time. Even then the guard merely slid the food through the slot near the floor, as was customary in most prisons. The freedom from interrogations and mistreatment was a welcome relief, and more so as he reveled in the glorious Presence of God in the prison-cell-turned-sanctuary. He could not remember any time before when God's Presence had become so real and his heart so full of joy.

Like the three disciples on the Mount of Transfiguration, he longed to just stay there alone with Jesus. During this time of the special ministry of the Holy Spirit to him, he sensed that God was about to do something unusual. What He would do, he had no idea, but day by day the assurance grew in his heart that in some mysterious way God was going to release him from prison.

If God sent His angel to deliver Peter from prison, could He not send one to deliver me? he thought.

Five days after Pastor Tan was led away to the labor camp, the cell door again creaked open and two guards entered.

"You are to appear before the judge today," they announced, as they helped Anching to stand. They led him slowly down the hallway to a larger room than he had seen before. Since his physical condition was so serious, he was offered a seat facing a long table. He waited, wondering what this was all about. After a few minutes, three men appeared and took their places at the other end of the table. One announced that this was a trial to determine what his sentence should be for breaking the law and holding unlawful meetings at which forbidden literature was distributed.

The proceedings moved along slowly as the judges looked at his papers, questioning him about his arrival in China and the purpose of his travels.

"You are a spy for the Taiwan Government," they repeatedly stated, "and you are a lackey of that imperialist paper tiger, the United States. You are spreading counter-revolutionary ideas among the people and circulating forbidden literature."

They're methodically building a case against me, he thought, as he listened attentively. *I fear that soon there will be no recourse but a long prison term.*

"There will be a recess for one hour," the lead judge stated.

"I understand you have great difficulty in walking. Is that correct?" he asked.

"That is correct, sir," Anching replied politely. "I have been severely beaten and…."

"You are not permitted to criticize the government authorities when you have broken so many laws of our country," the judge interrupted sternly. "Remain in your seat until we return," he stated with finality, as he and the other two judges rose to leave. The door closed behind them, and Anching was left alone with one guard. A strong sense of God's Presence invaded the room as he sat there. Psalm 91 had always been a favorite psalm of the Chinese believers, and they sang it regularly in times when they were pressed into a corner. Anching sang it softly now as he rested in the Lord, his refuge. The guard watched, not knowing what to make of this strange prisoner.

"He who dwells in the shelter of the Most High will rest in the shadow of the Almighty. I will say of the Lord, He is my refuge and my fortress, my God in whom I trust" (Psalm 91:1)

What comfort! What hope—even in the midst of this hopeless situation! His heart was greatly encouraged when he came to the verse, "A thousand may fall at your side, ten thousand at your right hand, but it will not come near you." He paused and reflected on that verse for some time.

"*Lord Jesus,*" he prayed, "*are You giving me a special message of deliverance from these judges and their decision?*" He picked up the song again and sang: "If you make the Most High your dwelling—even the Lord who is my refuge—then no harm will befall you, no disaster will come near your tent."

Anching's heart was lifted in praise to God at these wonderful promises. How God would fulfill His promises, he did not know, but he leaned more heavily on the Lord and continued to sing: "For he will command His angels concerning you, to guide you in all your ways."

He finished the psalm with the triumphant words: "He will call upon me, and I will answer him; I will be with him in trouble. I will deliver him and honor him." He sat quietly, meditating on these words of Scripture and enjoying the Presence of the Lord.

Fifteen minutes had elapsed as he reveled in God's Presence and Word. Suddenly there was a commotion out in the hallway. Loud shouting and running feet echoed through the building. *What's going on?* he thought, as he turned and looked at the nervous guard.

"What's happening?" he asked, finally. The guard moved toward the door, opened it, and listened. Clearly, shouts of "Fire! Fire!" were heard.

"The building is on fire," a guard shouted. "Get the prisoners out," called a voice. The hallway was rapidly filling with smoke as the guard stepped back and pulled the door shut. *What should I do?* he questioned as he looked around wildly.

"Get the prisoners out of their cells," the voice in the hallway shouted. *But where to?* The guard was clearly uncertain what to do in this unexpected crisis.

As the acrid smell of smoke filled the air and the shouting of commands continued, the door opened and in walked a high-ranking officer. Speaking to the guard, he ordered him to move quickly.

"I'm Officer Pao. I'll take charge of this prisoner. You run to the cells and help remove the prisoners. Keep them under guard at all times," he ordered. Anching sat quietly wondering what was happening.

As the relieved guard rushed out to follow orders, the officer turned to Anching and said with a commanding tone, "Follow me." Anching struggled painfully to his feet and shuffled after the officer. Slowly he followed, as the thick smoke caused him to choke and cough, along with all the others rushing here and there. No one paid any attention to him, except the officer who was leading him down the hallway. Painfully, he descended the steps to the lower floor, as the officer waited patiently for him.

"Stay close to me," the officer commanded, as the commotion increased. Reaching the lower level, the officer motioned him to turn to the right, leading Anching to the rear of the building, where there was a stampede of people attempting to exit the burning building. Raising his voice, he commanded their attention.

"I'm Officer Pao. Just move along in an orderly fashion and don't shove. We'll all get out." The reassuring voice seemed to quiet the fears of the crowd as all filed in an orderly fashion out of the building. Motioning to Anching, the officer led the way out to a narrow alley.

"Everyone," he ordered, "go to the main street to the left. That's right. Keep moving to safety." To Anching he said, "You go to the right. Keep walking out of the alley. Turn to the right. Keep walking, but do not run, until you come to a bicycle shop on the left. Go in and tell the first man you meet that Officer Pao said, "Take care of this man and help him. Do exactly as he instructs you. Now go!"

Without hesitating a moment, Anching walked slowly out of the alley and, as Officer Pao had instructed him, he turned right. Everyone else seemed to be running in the opposite direction in order to see the fire that was now spurting flames from ground floor windows. Slowly he made his way along the street, keeping watch for the bicycle shop.

Ah, there it is, he thought, as he approached the shop. Suddenly he paused, as he realized for the first time that he was free of the prison! Shocked, he looked around. *Is this a dream?* he asked himself.

The sound of sirens and shouting people brought him back to his senses. *I am free. Officer Pao must have been an angel sent from God to set me free,* he exulted joyously. He proceeded on to the bicycle shop and, upon entering, spoke to the only man in the place.

"Officer Pao sent me to you and said that you should help me."

The man did not appear surprised, but he looked into Anching's eyes for a moment, and then replied.

"Officer Pao sent you?"

"Yes," replied Anching. "He said I was to do whatever you told me to do."

"Quickly, follow me," he said urgently. "There's no time to lose. Start walking down this alley," he said, as he pointed the way. "I'll be with you in a moment." As Anching hobbled down the alley, the man went to a back room of his shop and spoke to his assistant.

"I'll be back shortly," he stated. A few moments later the shopkeeper caught up with Anching and led him out to another street.

"There's a believer's home not far from here where you can rest while I get a donkey cart to take you to a safer place."

Anching was glad for the chair that was offered him in the back room of the rice shop. Weary from the painful walk, he rested, while his new friend went for the donkey cart. In a few minutes, he returned and spoke to him.

"This man will take you to the farmer who will care for you until early tomorrow morning, when a truck with a load of rice will pick you up. It will transport you to Hubei Province, about fifty miles away."

"How did you know I want to go to Hubei Province?" Anching asked in surprise.

"I didn't," the man replied, "but I know you are a believer needing to escape to a safe place. The Hunan police do not cross into another province. Police from the different provinces don't cooperate with each other either, so I just figured that would be a safe place for you." Then, looking intently at Anching, he said, "Who are you, and who is Officer Pao?"

"You don't know Officer Pao?" Anching asked in surprise. "He told me to look for you!"

"I never heard of him before," the man replied, "but last night as I was meditating on God's Word, I was reading Acts 12 when I had a very strong sense that God wanted me to help the man who came into my shop asking for help. Now, you say, you don't know Officer Pao either?"

Anching briefly explained who he was and told of his deliverance from the burning building. The man just stood there staring at him.

"Then Officer Pao must have been an angel sent from God to deliver you," he exclaimed in surprise. "That's exactly what I was reading in Acts 12 about Peter being set free by the angel of the Lord! What you are saying is that God sent an angel to deliver you! Oh, praise the Lord. He has not changed one bit!"

"For a long time I have been quoting the verse from Hebrews that says 'Jesus Christ is the same yesterday, today, and forever'

(Hebrews 13:9)," Anching replied, "but today I realize more than ever before that it is true!"

"Come, Anching, this is all very exciting," the man replied, "but we are wasting time. I must get you concealed before the police discover you are missing. When they do, they will leave no stone unturned to find you. Here's what we will do. Get in this donkey cart and my friend will take you to a farm on the outskirts of town. About 4 A.M. a truck with a load of rice will pick you up and take you across the border into Hubei Province. You will be dropped off at a believer's rice shop. From there you can make your way on to your destination."

"How can I ever thank you for taking in a stranger like this? You are putting yourself at great risk for me."

"Do not thank me," the man replied. "I am only obeying the instructions of the Lord. And as for risk, we gladly give our lives each day for our Lord Jesus Christ, just as you do. Now, goodbye, my friend," the shopkeeper said, as he helped Anching into the donkey cart.

"And may God give you a safe journey!" A tarp was thrown over him and the owner prodded his old donkey into a slow walk down the road.

Back at the police station, bedlam reigned everywhere. Fire-fighters fought the blaze with the little equipment they had and finally began to bring the fire under control. The fire had started in the kitchen and spread rapidly through the old wooden building. It had threatened the lives of dozens of prisoners locked in their cells. Prisoners screamed for help. Some guards risked their lives to get the prisoners to safety. With the fire coming under control, the police chief began making a check of the prisoners. All were accounted for except one—Wen Anching was missing!

The guard on duty in the courtroom was questioned about his disappearance. "Officer Pao ordered me to go to the prisoner's cells and release the prisoners," he repeated over and over again.

"Well, who is Officer Pao?" questioned the chief. "There is no one here by that name."

"I never had seen him before," admitted the frightened guard, "but he spoke with such authority that I thought he must be from one of the other police stations that had come to help."

Other policemen came to the guard's rescue by testifying on his behalf.

"He was a very impressive officer," one policeman said. "He gave orders on how to evacuate the building, and everyone just followed his orders. There was so much confusion, but when he spoke, everyone listened. I believe many of us are here now because of that man, whoever he was."

"That's exactly what I saw," another policeman stated. "When that man spoke, everyone followed his instructions. I never remember meeting anyone quite like him," he said honestly.

"I don't care who Office Pao is or what he did. We have lost a prisoner, and I want him found or there is going to be trouble for all of you," the chief exploded in anger.

A half hour after leaving the rice shop, the donkey cart, with Anching hidden safely underneath the tarp, arrived at an isolated farm, where an elderly farmer welcomed them.

"I will bring you some food in a few minutes, young man. Then you must make a bed for yourself out here and get some rest. The rice truck will be by here about 4 A.M." Finishing his meal, Anching addressed the farmer.

"How can I ever thank you friends for risking your lives to help me?

"Anching," the older man replied, "someday the world will know that there were many Christians in China during the days of the Communist takeover. They will also discover, when the doors open again, that the believers were courageous followers of Jesus and willing to lay down their lives for Him. It has always been this way in China—way back to the time of the Boxer Rebellion. A lot of people gave their lives for Christ at that time, and there are a lot more today who would gladly lay their lives down for Him. We can't attend church any longer, but we still love and serve our Lord. If I live or die, it doesn't make any difference. I will follow Him all the days of my life, and someday I'll make it safely to my eternal home in heaven. So don't thank me for obeying Jesus. Let us both be faithful to the end."

A few minutes after making a comfortable bed on the fragrant hay, Anching fell soundly asleep. About 8 o'clock in the evening the farmer shook him awake.

"Hurry," he ordered. "A messenger just arrived saying that the police are out rounding up all known Christians for questioning. They have been here at my home before, and I'm sure they'll be back."

As he spoke a police van pulled up to his home, and several policemen hurried toward the house. Realizing the danger of the situation, the farmer whispered to Anching.

"Burrow down under the hay in that back corner." While Anching did as he was instructed, the farmer began to pile hay up in a mound. Then, rushing out to his house with a bag of rice, he encountered the police already inside his home.

"A dangerous prisoner escaped early this afternoon when a fire erupted in the police station. He is a religious fanatic who has been spreading illegal teachings about the government and our great leader. If you are hiding him here, you will be severely punished," said an officer gruffly.

"Hiding an escaped prisoner here?" he asked in surprise. "Look around. Our home is very small. There are no hiding places here!" The home was indeed very small, and it did not take them long to turn it upside down.

"Go look in the barn," the officer ordered when the prisoner was not found in the home. Rushing out, they saw the mound of hay and thought they had their man.

"Come out from under that hay," ordered the police officer, but there was no response. Seeing a pitchfork standing nearby, he shouted again.

"Come out from under that hay or I'll thrust this pitchfork right through you."

Anching hardly dared to breathe. He lay perfectly still in the corner and prayed. When there was no response to the officer's command, he raised the pitchfork and thrust it hard into the mound of hay. Over and over he thrust it into the mound and the area around it.

"He's not under there," he said with keen disappointment. "Come on," he said to the others, disgustedly, "we're wasting time. He's not here."

"That was a close one," the farmer said minutes later, as he gave Anching the all-clear signal. "The Lord has really sent His angels to protect you. Better make your bed in that corner for the rest of the night. It seems to be a pretty safe place, don't you think?" chuckled the farmer.

Chapter 14

AT LAST

T he rice truck heading into Hubei Province arrived at about
4 A.M.

"This is not going to be a very comfortable ride," the farmer
said, as Anching climbed up on top of the bags of rice. "Make yourself as comfortable as possible, and then we are going to arrange
the bags so you will be completely hidden. You won't be able to
get out until you reach your destination."

Thanking them all again, Anching settled down inside the dark
truck, as the rice bags were arranged to conceal him should they
be stopped for an inspection. They were on the road only a short
time when they were forced to stop at a police checkpoint.

"A very dangerous prisoner escaped yesterday," said an officer.
"We are checking all vehicles. Get out of the truck and stand over
there," he ordered, indicating where he wanted the driver and his
helper to stand. They searched the cab very thoroughly and, finding
nothing unusual, proceeded to open the back doors of the truck.
It was jammed full of rice bags.

"You've got a full load, don't you?" commented the officer as he shined his flashlight into the truck. "Doesn't look like you have room for an escapee," he said, closing up the doors again. "Keep your eyes open, and if you see this man, report it to the police immediately." He held up a large picture of Anching for the two men to see. "And, remember, there is a big reward for this criminal, dead or alive!"

They bounced along the dusty road as the sun peeped over the horizon. Anching's body ached from the rough ride, but his spirits surged as the men shouted in loud voices.

"We've just crossed into Hubei Province. Everything is going to be all right."

"Praise the Lord," came a faint echo from the back of the van. Although his body ached, Anching heaved a great sigh of relief. *If it is true that the Hunan police will not cross the border, then I really am free!*

Later, as he sat with his new benefactors, he was very much aware that he was following the cloud of God's Presence, and it had settled down once again—this time a few miles inside Hubei province.

"We are often tempted to choose the promises we want to hear," he told the Christian family who'd gathered together to hear his experiences. "But we are better followers of Jesus when we receive the entire Word of God, and not just the promises that sound sweet to our ears at the moment.

"In Hong Kong someone made a box of promises and each day we selected one from the box. I remember one day when a student selected a promise, and said with downcast face, 'I don't like this one. It's not what I want. Let me choose another one!' I remember our pastor admonishing us that we don't select the promise that gives us peace and security and sounds sweet to our ears. We accept the whole counsel of God even though sometimes He leads us through suffering and rejection. Even in times like that when we are not delivered in some miraculous way, God's Word sustains us and enables us to be victorious."

Anching continued sharing the testimony of his imprisonment and escape, and all rejoiced at the way God had healed his legs and then set him free from the prison.

"That's just like Peter being delivered in the Book of Acts," one of the men broke in excitedly. "And that encourages us to pray for the elder in the next town who was just arrested. We have not heard from him since he was arrested," he said, "but your deliverance encourages us to believe for him."

The family engaged in a period of fervent prayer for their elder to be bold and be able to endure whatever suffering was meted out to him by his cruel captors.

When the praying ceased, the head of the family addressed the group.

"Members of my family and of the household of God, will we follow the instructions of the police and cease to hold our meetings, or will we follow the Word of God?" He looked around at the family that was assembled and waited for their reply. As one body, they responded, "We will obey the Lord even though it means imprisonment or death!"

"Praise God," responded the head of the family. "We will follow the Lord because this world is not our home. We are bound for heaven and for eternity with our Lord."

During the next days Anching visited many house churches in the area, and in each place he recited Scripture, which was zealously written down by the believers. How they rejoiced when they read passages together, some for the first time in their lives.

"Please stay as long as you can," the people pleaded, "and give us more of God's Word." In each place, Anching instructed them to copy whatever Scripture they had and then pass it on to those without any.

"The Word of God is powerful," he instructed them, "and the Bible tells us that God's Word will not return void or empty, but will accomplish His purpose" (Isaiah 55:11).

Another year of chaos and confusion was ushered in, with only a slight lessening of the Red Guard movement. Chinese New Year, that occurs in February each year, was drawing closer. In spite of many difficulties, the house churches in the Taiping area were flourishing, and Meiling was kept busy. Since her last arrest, conditions had improved a little in the area and she continued her walks and house meetings whenever possible.

I have not celebrated New Year's with my family for years, she thought one day. *How I would love to be with them once again.* She also thought of Pastor Yang. *He has been in prison for almost twenty years. Maybe this is the year he will be freed,* she hoped. *And maybe this is the year Anching and I will meet again! It has been twenty-four years since he was taken into the army.*

A few days later, with some trepidation of heart, she walked to the police station and filled out a form for a travel permit to Puyang over Chinese New Year.

"You'll be notified within a week," the clerk said as she took the form, "but don't expect too much. There are very few permits being granted for the holiday."

When ten days had passed without any word from the police, Meiling decided to stop by and make inquiry. As usual, one expects to wait a very long time for officials to act on a simple request, and so it was for her now. Trying to be patient, she anxiously watched the movement of the man in charge, who seemed very busy shuffling the papers on his desk. Almost an hour passed before the clerk called her to the desk.

"You may go to the director's desk now," she said politely. Meiling walked over as confidently as she could, while attempting to hide her nervousness.

The director took his time in finding her application and then, looking at it for several seconds, lifted his head and spoke.

"Sorry, your application has been denied."

Did she hear him correctly? Application denied? But why?

"But sir," she began, "I just want to visit my elderly parents...."

"Application denied!" he interrupted. "That's all!"

She knew it was useless to make any further appeal. She turned, and with a heart that was breaking, walked slowly out of the police station.

Seated in the third-class section of the train to Puyang, Anching sensed an air of excitement everywhere. Chinese New Years was only two days away, and he was heading home. Anching rejoiced that the good people where he had been ministering for almost two weeks, had collected enough money for his train fare.

This is the last lap of the journey to my home, he thought with great joy. *And I will be a lot closer to Meiling! She's only three hundred miles north of Puyang, and once I arrive there, it will be easy to reach her!*

He dozed as the train rocked back and forth. These two weeks had been exhausting, with so much speaking and traveling, but he rejoiced that the Lord had opened so many doors, and many had prayed to receive Christ.

Suddenly he was awakened by a commotion at the front of the train. He heard harsh voices shouting. Three police officers were engaged in a heated conversation with a man whose travel documents were not in order. Everyone sat up rigidly, frightened that they could be harassed next. It was not unusual for the police to board the trains and inspect everyone's travel documents! Very frequently a passenger's papers were not in order. Sometimes they were put off the train and other times they were detained for further questioning. Anching's heart did a flip as he realized what was happening.

How was he going to fare with these officers? he wondered.

"Oh, Lord, I'm so close to home," he prayed silently. *"Help me through this one, too."*

As he nervously watched what was going on, the words of Scripture flashed into his mind: "Trust in the Lord with all your heart, and lean not unto your own understanding; in all your ways acknowledge Him, and He will make your paths straight" (Proverbs 3:5-6). Relieved, he sat watching, knowing that God had spoken again to him.

"I don't know what You're going to do, Lord," he said, *"but I'm waiting for Your surprise!"* Word filtered back quickly and quietly that the man up front was to be taken off the train for questioning at the next stop. A ripple of fear swept through the car as the police officers continued through the car, inspecting everyone's papers.

They were examining the papers of some students in the row ahead of Anching when one of them jumped to his feet and fled to the rear of the train. The three officers sprang into action, chasing after him. The young man bolted out the door toward the open platform of the old fashioned train and, hesitating only a few seconds, opened the gate by the steps and jumped off the moving train. The officers reached the platform too late to prevent his escape and stood looking back as they saw the man roll on the ground over and over again.

"There must be something wrong with his papers," one of the officers remarked.

"I'll bet he's banged up quite a bit,' another said, with a cruel laugh.

"Well, we can't do anything more about him," the first officer said with a shrug. "Let's get back to the rest of the passengers."

The shocked passengers looked at their newspapers or out the window, as the men came back down the aisle to continue their inspection. Anching's heart was racing, but he clung to his promise.

"I am Your child, Lord," he prayed. *"I'm ready for anything. Just give me all the wisdom and courage I will need to do it."*

Seated by the window, Anching concentrated on the passing farmland while the man next to him appeared to be studiously reading his newspaper.

"Now where were we," the lead man said as he approached Anching's seat. Stopping at the row behind Anching, he asked the man for his papers. With everything in order, he looked at the man next to him. Then, moving on back, they checked all the remaining passengers and proceeded to the next car. Anching continued looking out the window and the man next to him continued reading his newspaper, both trying to act nonchalant over being skipped in the inspection! Continuing to look out the window, Anching didn't see any of the passing scenery. Amazed at what had just happened, he bit his lip to keep from shouting his praise to God for yet another deliverance.

"Surely, Lord, I am kept in the hollow of Your hand. Blessed be the Name of the Lord!"

The steam engine puffed into Puyang station and Anching hurriedly rose to find his way home after an absence of twenty-four years. He knew no one would be there to meet him since no one knew he was anywhere near Puyang. Walking out of the station, which had changed very little since he had left years before, he made his way quickly down the street toward his parent's home three miles away. By the time he reached the familiar street, it was dark, but a little light shone in one of the windows of his old home. His heart was flooded with precious memories of his youth, his family, his conversion, and Meiling.

He paused to lift his voice in praise that he was finally home.

What a surprise this is going to be, he thought as he knocked firmly on the door. A voice called out.

"Who is it?" *Could that be his mother's voice?* It sounded old and weary, and maybe a little frightened with a late night visitor at the door.

"Mother," he called out, "it is Anching, your son!"

"Father," she screamed loudly, "come quickly. Anching is at the door." Fumbling with the bolt, she kept saying, "Anching is here. Anching is here!" Her husband rushed to the door and, taking away the plank that served as a bolt, he flung the door open and stared into the face of his son.

"Anching!" they kept saying as they hugged him and pulled him into the house. "Anching, you've come home at last!" his mother cried, wiping the tears from her eyes. "Oh, let me look at you," she cried. "Twenty-four years since they took you away! Oh, Anching, you look so good, so handsome!"

"Oh, what a great New Years we will celebrate this year," his father said, as he touched his son to make sure he was not dreaming.

Long into the night the three of them sat and talked about many things that had happened to the family. He learned about his brothers and sisters and the trials they had been through, and he rejoiced when his mother told him that each of them was a believer.

"We have all suffered for our faith, but we will never turn back," she said triumphantly. Mr. Wen agreed heartily, as Anching's eyes filled with tears of joy for his family.

"And have you any word about Meiling?" he asked at last.

"There has been no word from her for almost three months. The mail service is not very dependable," his mother explained.

"We have all been praying that she could return for New Years, but she has been denied a travel permit. Mrs. Woo is heartbroken. She had longed so much for a visit."

"I must visit her in the morning," Anching said in a husky voice. "Someday, in God's time, we'll all be together again," he reassured his mother. "I believe it, and I'm waiting for it," he said confidently.

In the morning, Anching reveled in the joy of being in his old home with his parents. There was so much to catch up on after twenty-four years of separation!

"Oh, praise the Lord that I lived long enough to see you again," his mother kept saying, as she dabbed at the tears that now flowed so easily. "God has been so faithful to all of us. When you left, your father was not a believer, and I was just a baby Christian. The years have been full of sorrow and pain, but it all has been worthwhile because the pain brought us close to Jesus."

"And I'm looking forward to the day when we will once again be able to attend a church and hear my son preach the sermon," father said proudly. "Yes, God has been so good to us. Even though we have lost almost all our earthly possessions, He has never failed us, and now He has even brought you back to us again."

"We'll need many weeks to catch up on all the past events of our lives," Anching said at last, "but now I want to go over and visit the Woo home and hear the latest news of Meiling. Twenty-four years ago I promised her I would come back for her, and that promise has kept me going all these years.

Walking along through an unfamiliar part of town to the apartment where the Woo family now resided, he thought of the pain and humiliation they had suffered for the cause of Christ. Imagine one of Puyang's most respected citizens living in one of the poorest neighborhoods of the city.

But, like his own parents and thousands of other Chinese believers who had been ravished by the Communists, he knew they would be rejoicing that they had been counted worthy to suffer with Jesus.

Reaching their neighborhood, he looked with dismay at the unkempt, dirty-looking row of tenement houses on both sides of the street. As the burgeoning population continued to increase at an alarming rate and factories had been erected, the Communist government had built basic housing as cheaply as possible. The strange odor hanging over the area testified to the fact that the hundreds of people crowded into these apartments had limited sanitary facilities. His heart went out to the Woo family, living in these unhealthy conditions. Locating their apartment house, he started climbing the narrow stairway to the third-floor apartment. The semidarkness of the hallway, reeking with the smell of urine, turned his stomach, especially as he remembered the glowing promises of the Communists that everything would be improved.

Walking down the third-floor hallway, he located the number of the Woo apartment, knocked on the door, and waited for a response. A woman's voice called out.

"Who's there?"

Could that be Mrs. Woo? he thought. *She sounds so tired and weary!* Responding softly, he answered her.

"Its Wen Anching," The door flew open as the surprised Mrs. Woo gasped in recognition. Speechless for a moment, she finally called out to her husband.

"Come quickly! Its Anching! He's returned at last!"

Pulling him into the apartment, she closed the door and just stood looking at him. When Mr. Woo hurried out, he gasped in shock. "Anching, is it really you?" Both hugged him as if he were their own son.

"Oh, how good to see you again," Mr. Woo said over and over. "I never thought I would live to see this day." Tears were flowing from Mrs. Woo's eyes as she tenderly wrapped her arms around him.

"Oh, thank You, Jesus. Blessed be your Name forever. He's come home at last!"

They talked of the Datung coal mine, Rennie's Mill Camp in Hong Kong, and of Anching's experiences of the past year as he had traveled north.

"God has been so good to all of us in spite of the worst things Satan has thrown at us," Mr. Woo said.

"Yes," Anching added, "we are more than conquerors through our Lord Jesus Christ (Romans 8:37). But tell me about Meiling. When was the last time you saw her? I can hardly wait to see her again."

"She is so anxious to see you again, too," Mrs. Woo said wistfully. "We have all been praying that she would be given permission to come home for Chinese New Years, but for some reason her request has been denied twice. And, now you are here! She will be so disappointed! The last time she was here she talked about you constantly. All of us have been praying that the day of reunion would come soon." Pausing, she added, "Ah, thank God, it is much closer now." She dabbed at her tears again, as she buried her face in her handkerchief and wept. "To think that my dear children have suffered so much and been separated so long," she said through her tears.

"Now mother," responded her husband tenderly, as he patted her arm, "through it all we have triumphed by the grace Jesus has supplied, and we will continue until the day when we see Him face to face." She smiled through her tears.

"Yes, praise the Lord. His grace has been sufficient."

"I must be going," Anching said at last. "Our families can visit over the holidays and worship together, even though there is no church open."

"The believers in our house church have been praying for you, and they will want to hear all the things God has done through you," responded Mr. Woo.

"Yes, we will get together in a day or so with your family. What a wonderful New Years gift you are, Anching!" he said, as he looked admiringly at him. "It could only be better if Meiling were here."

At that moment, a knock sounded at the door—not any ordinary knock, but the secret one the Woo family members always used to announce their arrival. Mr. Woo stiffened with surprise.

"That's our secret family knock," he said, as he moved toward the door. "I wonder. Who could it be?"

Opening the door, he gasped in surprise.

"Meiling! It's you!" Mrs. Woo was there in a second and drew her into the room and closed the door.

"Oh, Meiling," she said as she held her daughter close and wept. "How did you manage to get a travel permit?"

"That can wait, mother," said Mr. Woo. "Come, Meiling, see who else is here!" he said excitedly, leading her into the living room.

Hearing the name Meiling, Anching jumped to his feet just as Meiling entered the living room. Casting aside all Chinese culture and old taboos, they gazed into each other's eyes for only a second, and then rushed into each other's arms.

"At last, I have found you," Anching said as he held her close and hugged her.

"I can't believe it," Meiling responded. "What a miracle!"

Mr. Woo held his wife in his arms as she wept on his shoulder.

"We are reunited at last," he said, as he patted her head. "Oh, praise the Lord for His goodness to us."

"You are just as beautiful as when I left here twenty-four years ago," Anching kept saying as he gazed into Meiling's eyes.

"And you've grown more handsome than ever," she responded, holding his hands and looking long and deeply into his eyes.

Chapter 15

THE VISION FULFILLED

Meiling and Anching meandered down the pathway that led to the riverfront where they had first met many years before. Her one-month visit was almost over. Tomorrow she would return to Taiping. As Anching pulled the overgrown branches along the pathway aside to allow her through, Meiling looked at him with eyes brimming with love.

"I've been down this path many times since first we met here," she confessed. "I must admit that I've shed many tears on this rock. I never doubted that you would keep your promise, but after all that happened I have often wondered if you were still alive."

Anching took her hand in his and choked up as he replied.

"Meiling, the memory of those days when our love for each other was just budding kept me alive through many difficult situations. The hardest part for me also was wondering if you were alive, and not knowing what terrible sufferings you might be enduring. In spite of the awful circumstances, I clung to the hope that you were alive and that God would see you through every difficulty."

They sat side by side on the riverbank for a long time. Neither spoke as they contemplated that tomorrow they would again be separated. *Who knows, in these uncertain and perilous times, when we will meet again,* each was thinking.

Anching cleared his throat and, looking into Meiling's beautiful eyes said, "Meiling, you have been the focus of my life these many years. I dread the thought of being separated from you again."

"I feel the same way," she responded with deep emotion, "but at least we have found each other."

"True, but shouldn't there be more to life than this?" he replied, with some impatience in his voice. "How long must we endure this separation? I have wanted to marry you from the first time we sat here on this rock," he confessed again, with an embarrassed smile.

"It will only be as long as it takes to work through all the red tape of the government!" she responded with conviction, as she lowered her eyes and squeezed his hand tightly.

They both laughed as the tears fell on their clasped hands.

"But in reality," Anching responded softly, "I will never give up until that day arrives, and I will pray that it comes soon." Each was momentarily lost in thought, until Anching once again broke the silence.

"But, my dear Meiling, I don't know when that will be," he said wistfully. "And when it does happen, I cannot offer you much security. I am an itinerant preacher of the gospel, dependent on God alone for all my needs. I cannot offer you a beautiful home or even a secure income. In fact, I can only offer you the pain of separation and suffering that comes with the stand I have taken as a preacher and follower of Jesus Christ."

She squeezed his hand again and, with a brave smile, replied, "Anching, I settled that long ago. That's why I waited in confidence that you would keep your promise. I understand the cost of following Jesus in China today and the ever-present danger we both face as Christian leaders. But, come what may, we will stand together for Jesus and He will bless us; of that I am confident."

"I am haunted by the twenty years Pastor Yang was in prison for Christ's sake," he admitted honestly. "Maybe it is better ... " he said hesitantly as a startling thought crossed his mind. "Maybe it is better that we remain as we are. Even the Apostle Paul mentioned that because of the perilous times he lived in it might be better to remain unmarried."

"No!" Meiling replied vehemently. "No! I believe God has preserved us to serve side by side. We will wait patiently for the Lord's timing, and I believe He will open the way."

Still holding hands, Anching prayed for the removal of government restrictions and questions about his permanent residence in the land.

"And until that day, dear Lord," he prayed, "we will wait for You to open the way, and we will go on loving each other."

"I must leave tomorrow," Meiling said sadly as they stood to go. "These moments have been indelibly impressed on my heart. I will never forget them. I only pray that we can be joined together as soon as possible."

"Believe me," Anching responded, "I will not rest until every hurdle has been cleared."

The next morning both families and many Christians gathered at the railway station to say goodbye to their beloved Meiling.

"I will plan to visit Taiping as soon as possible," Anching whispered as Meiling prepared to board the train. "God has brought us together again, and He will complete the work. We will trust Him to unite us in marriage soon." With tears in her eyes she boarded the train and headed back to Taiping.

Making application to remain in China so he could marry Meiling became Anching's highest priority. During the next two months, while he impatiently waited for his resident papers to be approved, he visited the Christians in several towns and strengthened them in the Word. In every place he urged people to copy down Scripture passages and to make their own handwritten Bibles.

"It is by the Word of God that we are nourished, and without it we will be ignorant of how to live for Christ in this evil world," he told everyone. "On the other hand, it is also dangerous to be found with any kind of Scripture in your possession," he warned, "but it is the risk we must take in order to be faithful followers of our Lord."

How he longed for another mimeograph machine! He was amazed as he observed the passion the believers had for copying down Scripture to make their own Bibles. The effect on their spiritual lives was astounding, and almost overnight they were growing spiritually and making great strides in obedience to the Word of God.

Getting permission to marry was more complicated than either Anching or Meiling had imagined. With a paranoid government constantly decreeing new laws that controlled every aspect of people's lives, it was difficult to get permission to live and work in the same city. Exhausted from long hours of seeking employment for weeks on end, Anching was relieved when he finally found a job in a shoe factory in the nearby city of Wuhan. He was now one step closer to realizing his desire to marry Meiling.

Twenty years of crushing stone in a stone quarry in a reeducation program had left an indelible mark on Pastor Yang of the Puyang Church. As he packed his few belongings and prepared to leave the barracks that had been his home for those long years, he was filled with pain at the thought of leaving the many Christian prisoners. So many had found their way to Christ through his consistent ministry of compassion and love.

Oh, how I wish I could have held worship services for these dear brothers *in Christ,* he thought, as he finished packing his small bag. *Even though these men had come to Christ and been transformed, they had never experienced a congregation at worship. And when I get back to my home,* he thought, *there will be no church to attend—only small, secret house churches that exist in the fear and shadow of possible police raids at any hour.*

As he fell into line for breakfast, man after man nodded to him or gave a cautious hand signal of thanks. One man standing behind him whispered to him.

"Thank you for bringing Christ to this hole. As a result of your testimony, He changed my life."

Tears clouded Pastor Yang's eyes as the men whispered a word or gave a hand signal.

"I'll meet you in heaven," he whispered quietly.

"*As much as I want to leave this place,*" Pastor Yang prayed, "*these are my brothers in Christ, my family. Oh God, bless them, and send them someone who will help them through the dark hours of their imprisonment.*"

With breakfast finished, the men formed the familiar, long lines and marched off to the quarry. Pastor Yang stood watching them walk out of his life.

"OK, Yang," a guard spoke up, "it's time to go." Then, softening his tone, he spoke again. "You really feel for these men, don't you? You're the first pastor I have ever met. I must say I don't think I will ever forget you."

Courageously, Pastor Yang replied with a sincere smile that spoke volumes to the guard. "I'm not the important one. Jesus is." He picked up his small bag and followed the guard to the front office, where he signed some documents and then was pointed to the door and ushered out. The sound of the prison door clanging shut behind him as he stood in this strange world outside of the prison, sent a shiver up his spine.

Free, he thought, *but what does that mean? I'm still a prisoner in this land, only there are no bars on the windows now.*

He walked to the train station and purchased his ticket to Wuchang and his village of Puyang.

As the train pulled into the Wuchang station, his wife strained her neck to find him among the many disembarking passengers. Both wondered what the other looked like. Only twice in twenty years had she been allowed to visit him for a few minutes at the prison. Stepping off the train, he looked around, searching, until he saw a woman waving her hand. Their eyes locked for a few seconds as they searched their memories for the faces they had known so long ago. Breaking into wide smiles they pushed their way forward, and for a few seconds, grasped each other in a strong embrace.

"At last!" they both exclaimed, as the tears rolled down their cheeks.

"At last. Oh, thank God. At last!"

They had much to talk about, and so they sat hour after hour, sharing the news of the years but always returning to one central thought. In spite of everything that had happened, it had been worthwhile to suffer for Jesus, and they would do it all over again if necessary.

Although twenty years of the repressive regime of Mao Zedong had brought China to the lowest depths of despair, and the Puyang Church was still closed and used as a storage center, Pastor Yang's release from prison sent a wave of hope through every believer's heart. As he moved among the believers, he encouraged them by sharing the many experiences of his prison days. He and Mr. Woo understood better than most of the people the depth of despair that seizes the heart of those in prison.

"Brother Woo," he said one day, "the hand of our God has been on your life, and heaven will be enriched by the converts from the

Datung mines. I often prayed for you, even though I knew nothing about your circumstances."

"I also learned the joy of praying for you and many others," Mr. Woo responded. "Pastor Wong was so much like you, and he taught me much as a young believer. I could never have made it without either of you."

"And Anching, what a joy to meet you again," Pastor Yang said, looking into the eyes of the man he had prayed for time after time during the past twenty years. "You were in my prayers often, but I had no idea how God was using you. Someday soon I want to share with you the vision God has given me for Central China. I think perhaps you would like to be part of God's plan to prepare many young people to reach China and the world."

"We must meet soon," Anching replied with enthusiasm. "I will have a difficult time waiting to hear what God has revealed to you."

One morning a few days later Pastor Yang spoke to his wife as they paused to pray together. "A number of years ago when I felt very discouraged, God spoke to me and gave me a great vision for the years left to me when I would be released from prison."

She looked at him, wondering what he was about to share with her, but waited until he spoke.

"God showed me very clearly that while I was in the prison I was to do everything I could to win men to Christ, and I did. When I left there a few days ago, there were dozens and dozens of men who signaled their thanks for helping them find Christ. But God also gave me a vision for the future."

He paused as he watched the effect of his words on his wife. She sat quietly waiting, without comment or indication of the sudden fear that crept up into her throat. She sensed in that moment that he had not changed over the years. His first concern, as always, was to reach others for Christ.

Slowly he began to speak.

"I hesitate to tell you this because it could be very dangerous and cause more separation for us. You have been through so much already. I have struggled with this issue many times through the years but, my dear wife, I can do nothing else than obey my Lord."

Looking him directly in the eye she replied with deep emotion, "Do you remember, years ago, when we sat in that first meeting with the Communist officials? I told you I would rather be a widow than be married to a coward who denied his Lord."

"Yes," he responded, "and after I took my stand I eventually went to prison for it."

"That's right, you did, and I have been so proud of you and of your stand. I don't know what your vision is, but I will stand by you in the future, as I have these past twenty years, no matter what the cost. Together we will always walk the pathway that God lays out before us."

His throat choked with emotion as he took his wife's hand in his own.

"My dear wife, you have not changed either. Jesus is still supreme in your life. God will help us and will see us through whatever lies ahead. Here's what I must do. In the next weeks and months I must seek out several young people who love the Lord. They will be people who love Jesus with all their hearts and who are not afraid of dying for Jesus. God wants me to begin a Bible School to train these young people to take my place." He paused and watched his wife's expression.

"Would you believe me when I say that long ago I settled this issue with God?" exclaimed his wife. "I promised Him that when you were released I would assist you in every way to do just that."

Looking long into his wife's lovely eyes, he knew she was really saying, "I'm also ready to die for Jesus." They shared in prayer together, realizing that through the years God had prepared them for this moment. He had given each of them the same vision and both had made their own commitment to pay any price to see the church in China grow for the glory of God. In those moments together, God came down and bathed their hearts with His love and joy.

"We will begin with a small group," he continued as they finished praying, "and meet quietly, without fanfare. We will wait for God to send us the people He has prepared for future leadership. In time, we will witness the birth of a Bible School that will touch this nation and the world for God.

"Something else God showed me while I was in prison," Pastor Yang continued. "He showed me that the Chinese Church would one day rise up to become a great missionary-sending church that would reach out to the lands surrounding us that are bound in darkness. One day He will raise up a great army of people who will take the gospel westward through the Buddhist, Tibetan, and Muslim countries until His Name is known everywhere."

"You are an old man," his wife reminded him with a twinkle in her eyes, "but I see that your vision has not dimmed. I believe your greatest work is still ahead of you. I pray that we can do it together for His glory."

Sitting down together in Pastor Yang's tiny apartment, Anching listened attentively as his friend outlined his vision to train young people for ministry, even in the dangerous times that prevailed.

"Anching," he said, leaning forward to look him in the eye, "would you be willing to join me in this adventure of faith? Would you be willing to put your life on the line for God and to accept a call to be part of this vision?"

Anching didn't blink as he responded.

"Pastor Yang, I am a young man with a passion to reach China with the gospel and, through Chinese Christian workers, to reach the world. I would count it a great privilege to join you in preparing many young people for ministry."

"I must ask you one more question," Pastor Yang said seriously. "Are you prepared to be separated from Meiling and perhaps go to prison again? Are you ready for hardship and privation, and possible death?"

Slowly the full consequences penetrated Anching's heart as the pastor asked these penetrating questions. *Am I willing to be separated from Meiling?* The question struck him like a knife in his heart. *I have waited twenty-four years to be with her again, and now he is asking me to give her up! Go to prison again?* His mind reeled. *Am I ready to follow Jesus to death?*

Anching bowed his head as these thoughts swirled through his mind. *Yes, I love Jesus with all my heart, but more separation, more prison? Lord, is that what You are asking of me right now?* he questioned. The battle raged in his heart for a few moments that seemed like years. *Haven't we suffered enough already? Lord, would You ask more? Would You ask me even to give up Meiling now that I have found her?* These thoughts rushed through his mind. That old deceiver pressed him hard again, reminding him of his years of sacrifice and suffering.

"Anching," the tempter's voice rose a notch. "*Anching, think it over!* he urged. *You're not even married yet, and he's talking about giving her up! Don't be a fool. I warn you. You've sacrificed enough.*"

The words of Scripture rushed to his mind: "Anyone who does not take up his cross and follow me is not worthy of me" (Matthew 10:38). But Satan came right back with another stabbing thought.

"*Throw your lot in with this man and you'll go to jail again. I guarantee it!*"

"*Love the Lord your God with all your heart and with all your soul and with all your mind and with all your strength,*" Jesus gently spoke to his heart. *"My son, 'what good will it be for a man if he gains the whole world, yet forfeits his own soul?'"* (Mark 8:36).

Pastor Yang watched anxiously as this titanic struggle raged in Anching's heart. How well he knew the price to be paid and the years of separation and suffering that a decision to surrender to Christ like this demanded.

"Lord," he prayed silently, *"protect him in this moment of temptation."*

Raising his eyes slowly, Anching looked unflinchingly at the pastor. Tears filled his eyes as he reached out and took the pastor's hand and, ever so slowly, whispered, with deep emotion choking his voice. "Pastor Yang, with God's help…," he paused and took a deep breath. "With God's help, I will follow Him…all the way— regardless of the cost."

"The price is extremely high, Anching," the pastor said softly, as tears filled his own eyes, "but you will never regret it. While I cracked rocks in prison, I prayed for you, even though I had no idea where you might be. I claimed you for God's work—a young man to help this old man fulfill the vision God had given me."

Clasping hands, they prayed together, confessing their weakness and their fear of personal loss and separation.

"Yes, Lord," they prayed, *"we will follow where You lead us and we will be faithful unto death."*

The weeks of waiting seemed like eternity. Anching visited the immigration office as frequently as time permitted and begged the clerks to check on his application. Finally, one day as he returned from work, he learned that his residency papers had been approved. The last hurdle had been cleared, and he was now free to proceed with his plans to marry Meiling! He could hardly contain himself. He felt like shouting his praises to God out loud!

With his residency papers in hand, it would be easy to get a marriage license. At last his promise made to Meiling twenty-four years earlier was about to be realized. He thanked God for His timing. Another answer to prayer came a few weeks later when Meiling was granted permission to relocate to Puyang.

For Anching, the days of waiting for her arrival were the longest ones of his life.

Yes, he thought, with thanksgiving in his heart, *all these many years Meiling and I have been exiles with the burning hope that one day we would be joined together in marriage. At last, it is about to be realized, but we must never forget that we are still exiles of hope in a world that is not our home.*

MORE BOOKS BY THIS AUTHOR

Books for General Readers

To China and Back (An autobiography)
Giants Walked Among Us (The Story of Paul and Ina Bartel)
Red Runs the River:
The Story of China's Persecuted Church, Volume One

Christian Mystery Books for Children:

The Jack and Jenny Mystery Series:
- Smugglers in Hong Kong
- Capture of the Twin Dragon
- Mystery of the Counterfeit Money
- Rescue at Cripple Creek
- The Tiger Shark Strikes Again
- Coming Soon – Hijacked!

Missionary Books for Children:

Japan: Land of Great Surprises
Adventures on the Star of Suez

*Book descriptions and how to obtain them are found
on the author's web site:*

www.bollback.com

Or

by contacting him by e-mail.

*All of the books for adults are also available on Amazon.com
and Barnesandnoble.com*

Reader feedback is welcome at:

email: Kahu@juno.com

To order additional copies of

EXILES
OF HOPE

Have your credit card ready and call:

1-877-421-READ (7323)

or please visit our web site at
www.pleasantword.com

Also available at:
www.amazon.com
and
www.barnesandnoble.com

Printed in the United States
47857LVS00004B/184-231